The Harvest

BY

Kevin D. Young

Best wishes to you Carol —

9/13/11

Kevin D. Young

INFIΩITY
PUBLISHING.COM

ISBN 0-7414-5430-0

Published by:

INFINITY
PUBLISHING.COM

1094 New DeHaven Street, Suite 100
West Conshohocken, PA 19428-2713
Info@buybooksontheweb.com
www.buybooksontheweb.com
Toll-free (877) BUY BOOK
Local Phone (610) 941-9999
Fax (610) 941-9959

Printed in the United States of America

Published July 2009

Table of Contents

Preface

Ever have an experience so hellish that your nightmares are a welcomed relief? I've had such an experience. It is the sort of experience that has left me emotionally paralyzed and psychologically warped; the kind of thing that sends you groping for sanity, but finding none. I've long since been fully aware of the treachery of man, but never in my wildest imagination could I have constructed the hideousness of my story. It has completely changed and utterly destroyed my life forever.

Welcome to my nightmare—

Welcome, to "The Harvest..."

Chapter 1

"The Bloody Tree Stump"

Smack! A stiff slap stung across my face.

"Who the fuck do you think you are, you little piss ant? I think I'm gonna tear you a new asshole for buttin into other folks business," shouted Petee.

My hands were tied behind my back, and I had been at their mercy for what seemed like an eternity. I could no longer see out of my left eye, and my ribs hurt something awful. The entire group was drunk. Stumbling around smoking weed, cursing and yelling, they were having themselves a good old time. At first, I counted a dozen or so, soon the number grew to over fifty. I couldn't believe what was happening, but there I was on my knees and tied to a tree stump. They rode circles around me on their bikes and threw their empty beer bottles and cans at me. Most hit the stump, but the flying glass tore at my face, head and neck. Sometimes the bottles hit me in the back, but that didn't hurt nearly as much as the half-empty cans that managed to crash against my head. They cheered loudly when that happened. I prayed that God would spare my life so that I could take theirs.

My resolve was strong, as I swore that if I lived through this nightmare, I'd spend the rest of my life tracking and killing every one of them. The roar of the circling bikes was deafening as the dust and dirt swirled in every direction. I could barely see, but when I did crack my eyelids, they burned badly from blood, beer and dirt. The roar began to die down, and the cloud of dust began to settle. The once bright blue sky turned navy and my view had grown dim. They began forming a circle around the stump with their headlights pointed directly at me. Coughing and wheezing and puking my brains out, I raised my head for a second— a real mistake. Out of nowhere came a blow to the back of my neck that sent spikes of shock waves through my whole body. My tongue was completely dry and swollen. My throat tasted of dirt and dried blood.

"Thirsty, are you boy? You want something to wash that dirt off your tongue? Answer me," he yelled. Exhausted and reeling with pain, I nodded weakly.

He walked back to his bike grabbed a canteen and stumbled back. He screwed off the cap and took a swallow. Taunting me, he leaned down and belched in my ear. Then he poured the rest on top of the stump. The water splashed off and trickled down the sides of the trunk. I tried to catch part of the run off. "You want something to drink? I'll give you something to drink." With a wide and evil grin, Petee reached down and unzipped his fly. Reaching into his pants he grabbed his dick and said, "I'll give you something to drink all right." Holding himself, he walked closer to me. From less than a foot away he said, "Drink this." This sick, sadistic son of a bitch started pissing on me; in my face, on my head, everywhere. Then a few of his buddies joined in. The warm salty urine went up my nose, and in my mouth. My flesh was on fire as it seeped into the cuts on my face, arms and head. I couldn't even cry out. Utterly stunned, I knelt there in shame and disbelief. *How can something so horrible be happening to me?*, I thought. *My God, what about Christine?* I prayed to God that she had gotten away. Soaking wet and dripping with the stench of urine, I began to sob like a baby. I was broken, and it didn't matter who knew.

"Shut up bitch. Look at you, crying like a little bitch," someone shouted. I was far beyond caring about words; my pain was too great.

"Now what would that cute little whore of yours say if she saw you crying like a bitch?"

I thought about how much I loved Christine. We had just been married last fall. I thought of her playful smile and gentle touch. The thoughts warmed my heart, and for a split second, I was no longer there cradling that tree trunk.

Suddenly, a loud sound of spinning tires brought me back, front and center, and the nightmare continued. Out of the corner of my eye, I could see an old ratty van pulling up to a clearing among the bikers. The van turned hard to its right and an object came hurling out of the opened back doors. Again, I squinted in an effort to focus on the object, when everything inside me went cold. Bloody and naked with her hands tied behind her back, it was my baby girl. It was Christine. Her mouth was gagged, and even in the dim light, I could see that her body was bruised from head to toe. This soft and delicate creature was now a contorted mass of beaten flesh. I no longer felt the pain of my cuts and bruises. Hate consumed me and nothing cuts deeper. I erupted with a barrage of obscenities, vowing to kill everyone there. I twitched and struggled to free myself, but it was no use. "Keep your ass still peckerhead, she ain't dead yet. In fact, we ain't going to kill her until everybody is done fuckin her. What the fuck made you think you could keep such a fine piece of ass all to yourself, boy? You know, he said, "that there little missy of yours can sure cook. She ain't worth a hill of beans now, but I got to hand it to you— that pussy used to be the best. I was first you know. Everybody else was satisfied too, but then again, I stopped asking after the sixteenth man in line got himself a piece. That's right boy, damn near twenty good old boys fucked your woman. What do you think of that?"

I was totally vacant. The horrors she must have endured. I thought for sure that I'd finally reached bottom and for the first time in my life, I eagerly welcomed death. Suddenly, I felt the chains around my wrist drop to the ground. *Thank God*, I thought. I was finally being freed. They shouted for me to stand but I couldn't move. My body was not responding. It was as if I was frozen on my knees. They dragged me up and over the stump, slamming me down hard. I found myself gasping for air while staring directly at the ground, praying that it would be over soon. In the light sand at the base of the stump, I began to notice two small, yet swelling pools of liquid. I watched as they continued to grow in size. Finally, I realized that blood was generously dripping from the tips of my fingers. I followed the blood with my eyes from the puddles to my fingertips, to the palms of my hands and up my arms. The sides of the stump were sticky with blood, as the generous flow raced over the edges of the stump's jagged surface. Funny thing, I hadn't even realized that I was lying face down across a bed of broken glass; it took the sight of the puddles in the sand to fill me in. I felt the blood oozing from my body, although it wasn't as painful as I thought it might be. It mostly felt like I was leaking. Like a human inflatable doll about to deflate completely, I continued to wither. My troubles seemed to be lessening, too. Who would have thought it— the closer I got to death, the better I felt. Ironically, if I fought to stay alive, the pain was greater. While musing in my mind of the sweet serenity of death, I closed my eyes and waited. But it wasn't over.

New shackles were thrown to the ground. They chained my wrists to the stump. Then a new set of chains was tightly clasped around my ankles, which were then chained to my wrists. I couldn't move one inch in any direction. I tensed as they cut away my pants leg. The veins in my temples pulsated, as my remaining sensibilities told me what was about to happen. Everything that happened up until now slowly began to leave my mind. I had to prepare myself for the unthinkable.

Feeling the coolness of a blade against my skin, it tore and sliced my pants free from my body. I could hear rumbles of laughter and excitement coming from what sounded like a herd of animals. Anguished and tormented, I fought vigorously with myself. *Is a man still a man after another man has forcibly entered him?* I questioned. My body shook with uncontrollable fear. *Please, God let me die— let me die,* I prayed silently. *Maybe I'm dead and I'm in hell. Will I continue to die over and over, one death more horrible than the previous one?* My pants and underwear were cut to shreds, as they fell silently to the ground. With my eyes now firmly fixed on Christine's lifeless body, I waited. *My God, I pray that you will be merciful and end this nightmare.* As I lay there bracing myself with my eyes still fixed on Christine, I noticed some movement. *Dear God, why must we endure so much?* I cried. *I'll take this madness, just please God take her with you, please.*

She began coughing up blood as she slowly tried to move her limbs. Beginning to cry she called out to me. Helplessly, she laid in the dark sand as she tried to cover up her nakedness. She still had her pride. *I've never loved her as much as I do at this very moment,* I thought. As she desperately tried to cover herself with dirt and debris, I noticed a few of the female bikers began to turn away. Balling herself into the fetal position, she quietly cried in defeat. My eyes were glued on my beloved. She was now the only thing that mattered in the universe. Just then she looked up at me. Realizing the hideousness of my situation, her expression was one of disbelief. I followed her eyes as she surveyed my predicament. Her hazy stare rolled down to the chains around my wrists and ankles and up to the sight of my bare ass; the horror my position revealed. Her face, now wearing the expression of stark terror turned petrified. I knew that she was totally consumed with my pain, and me, totally forgetting her own. That look, I knew that look. It had to be identical to my own. Finally her eyes met mine and they told me how she wished she could take away my pain. I, too, spoke the same with my eyes. She managed to crack a faint shadow of a smile and mouthed the words "I love you." No longer trying to fight back the tears, my heart melted with the bitter- sweet pain of the moment. Now flushed with a deep sense of pride and admiration, I vowed to survive this ordeal. I mouthed back to her, *I love you so much.* I was able to feel my baby just one last time and at that moment, I felt her all over. I thought, *what ever happens now, we are together. Our spirits have been joined, and no one can take that away.*

Consumed with our connection, I hadn't realized that this extremely rowdy bunch had grown strangely quiet. As I refocused on Christine, I saw that her arm was outstretched in my direction. I screamed a cry of helplessness, as I stretched my hands in her direction. Apparently this was too much for one of the female biker's, as she stepped into the center of the ring and dropped some clothes at Christine's feet. "Put these on," she said. Then she looked over at me, then back at Christine and with a surprising amount of compassion she whispered, "I'm so sorry." She marched back to her bike and said, "This is bullshit man, I'm out of here." With that she started up her bike, motioned to a few others and rode off into the night.

"Don't mean shit dickhead, your ass still belongs to me. Since your dirty little whore seems so worn out and all, we gonna do you in her place, how's that sound to you?" he said.

Out of the crowd someone shouted, "Not me man, I ain't into this homo shit. You are one sick bastard." Kicking around a few beer cans, he motioned to a few others. Mumbling, cursing and grabbing for helmets, a half dozen or so kick-started their noisy bikes, and rumbled their way from the scene. Perhaps this Pete character sensed his party was waning, so he decided to make it interesting. He got down on his knees and looked me directly in the face. He said, "Hey boy, I'll give you a choice and I give you my word that I'll stick to it.

"You can either watch me and my boys fuck your whore until she's dead, or you can have the privilege of being fucked by a real man."

He stood up and informed everyone of the choice that he had given me, and said he'd give me a minute to think it over.

I looked out into the sea of spoke wheels and headlights trying to make out the faces of those perched on top of the bikes. I could see the evil drain from some of their

7

faces, as our eyes met and locked. I continued my penetrating stare, as some were forced to turn away. They seemed to be wearing the faces of ashamed little boys. One after another, I searched for the look of unchangeable evil that had to exist in their hearts. The features of their faces will stay permanently seared in my mind, yet the look in their eyes, curiously enough, evoked sympathy from my heart. I even saw tears in one man's eyes, and for one split second, I thought there may have been more than just two victims here. It was then that I knew I still had some humanity left. Finding more and more reasons to live, I stared into the swelling pool of tears in his eyes and shouted, *"You've soiled my wife, broken our bodies and completely shattered our spirit, but I love that woman more than my life. I'm already dead inside. You all have killed me. Spare her and do what you will to me, but remember that I am still a man and nothing you do will take that away from me. Think about that, when next you call yourselves men."*

With eyes still fixed on the man with tears, I watched as if in slow motion as a tear spilled out of the corner of his eye and onto his cheek. He stepped forward still looking me straight in the eye and said with a frown as he spun around to the sea of headlights, "That's it! It's over. This shit has to stop somewhere. Everybody get your shit and let's roll."

"Hell no," shouted Petee. "I don't give a shit about him and I definitely don't give a shit about his sissy little words."

"I'm gonna tell you one more time," shouted the man with the freed tear, "This is bad and this scene is over."

Gesturing, he shoved Petee slightly, in the direction of his bike. All the while, I thought Petee was the leader. It turns out that the man with tears was truly the leader. Petee said that nobody was gonna stop him. He stormed back to his position behind me and began to undo his buckle. Slapping me hard on the rump, he bellowed loudly, like some wild animal preparing to mount its bitch. The man

8

with tears shook his head, then looked up at Petee and said, "So this is the way you want it?"

Petee replied, "This is the way I'm gonna have it."

He pulled down his zipper and I heard his studded leather pants hit the ground. I looked up at the man with the tear. He looked up and past me, then slowly nodded his head up and then down. I couldn't believe he was giving Petee the go ahead. Right then, I knew my life was about to change forever. Lowering my head in defeat, I clenched my teeth, bracing myself. Then suddenly a shot rang out piercing what was once an eerie silence. As the sound of the shot echoed in the distance, Petee collapsed. Crashing down on my back, he rolled off the side and fell motionless to the ground. His eyes were fixed and open, and staring straight into mine. The monster, it seemed, was dead. Yet somehow Christine and I were still alive. Without speaking another word, the man with the tears walked over to his bike, reached into a leather saddle-bag and took out a hammer and chisel. One of the greatest sounds of my life was to hear the shackles drop to the ground for the last time. After he broke the wrist and ankle restraints, he removed the leather pants from Petee's body and laid them next to the stump. First covering me with a towel, he dragged Petee's body off into the bushes. He and another biker helped me to my feet and placed me nearer to Christine. I couldn't walk and could barely move my arms, but I clawed at the sand and dirt to get to my Christy. I put my hand in her limp palm. *Surely she's dead*, I thought. Then to my surprise she weakly wrapped her fingers around my hand. Bursting into tears, I pulled myself closer to her. She opened her eyes, and we pulled each other closer with all the strength we had left. Bloody and filthy, we laid in the sand holding each other, assuring ourselves that it was going to be alright. As we hugged and kissed and cried, the roar of the remaining dozen or so motorcycle engines sputtered off into a huge cloud of dust.

When the dust cleared all that remained was Christine and me, the stars, the moon glow, and that battered, bloody tree stump. Still cradling her in my arms, I looked down at her tiny hand in mine— like caramel in chocolate. I wiped away some blood from her beautiful dark face and thought, *how can this still happen? In a modern, and enlightened society that is supposed to be past this level of bigotry, how?*

As my eyes began to close, I could faintly hear the rustling of small animals in the brush...

Chapter 2

"Coma"

In a panic, I clenched my fists in defiance of something, perhaps the unknown. With my arms at my sides, my eyes fluttered open. I couldn't see very clearly. What I did see sent flames of stark terror through my stomach. I lay there still as stone. Furiously, I tried to blink for clarity, but I could only manage a few limited winks. The burning terror in my stomach began to build.

Can it be? I thought. *I'm not ready yet. No. I refuse to go. Please, let me up. It's not time for me yet. I lived through hell just for this? No, this can't be right. I lived, didn't I?*

I still couldn't move, feeling almost nothing. Tears overflowed their banks, spilling out of the corners of my eyes. I knew I was looking at something, but what, I wasn't sure. It was either glass or some kind of plastic. Whatever it was, I was completely surrounded by it and it seemed to be less than a foot from my face. My heart ached as if punctured with a dagger. The dagger was the realization that I was in a long, glass coffin. As I lay, I felt fear and terror bleed from my body. Everything that had ever happened to me that conjured up fear and pain flashed before my eyes. At lightning speed, I relived every inadequacy and insecurity of my life. It was as if my nervous system had just imploded. Everything was all over the place and control was not a functioning term in this existence. While I was getting a grip on my coming apart, guilt began to make a strong showing. Shame, as well, decided to join the cast of squalid characteristics. One by one, the memories whisked past like shooting stars, each one leaving behind its thorny reminder that everything in life costs something. The journey continued for what seemed like forever. Eventually this orgy of torment began to lessen, until it finally gave way to the warmth of peaceful bliss.

I've finally passed on, I thought. *Thank God, I've finally passed on.* The images turned soft and pleasant. There were no more tears of sorrow. My fists were unclenched and relaxed, and lay at my side. A hint of warm light cascaded down the full of my face, and the air was velvety cool. Finally, I'd been freed. Feeling myself slip away from myself, I settled down for travel and gave in to the moment. As if my body was floating through mid-air, I remained adrift. Helplessly floating and drifting, I began to soar over the earth, looking down on all that I used to be. I recognized nothing, but felt quite comfortable with everything. I knew this had to stop somewhere, but linear time was not easily measured. When next I returned to what seemed like reality, again I was immobile and unable to clearly make out what was encasing my body. I was still quite groggy, but soon became aware that I was lying not in a coffin but a bed. The mattress was soft but quite firm. Colors didn't register, except for white. At least that was as much as I could see through the plastic that covered my bed. My eyes were busy reprogramming my brain, ensuring that it understood I was in a bed and not a coffin. This outer covering was some sort of plastic or glass protection that fully enclosed my body. Indeed, I was still alive!

Faintly, I could hear a commotion off to my left. It seemed that I was in a hospital. I could hear the sound of talk over the intercom. It wasn't clear, but it was constant and full of short spurts of dialogue ending with the term, stat! The talk was loud now. *Someone must have opened a door,* I thought. Voices were coming from inside the room, coupled with the sound of latches being undone, from under the bed. A few snaps and zippers and the cover was lifted. Now clearly visible were the faces of angels all dressed in white. The subtle curves of their faces told me they were kind and gentle, but gave no indication of gender. Busily they connected and disconnected wires while changing my dressings. The outer covering was removed completely and steel bars were raised on both sides of the bed. They looked down at me, but I couldn't make out any expression. One of them reached over, and pulled a thick leather strap over my chest. Doing the same for my legs, my body was fully restrained. Through it all, I could feel nothing, but I could hear almost everything. They were preparing to move me.

"What a shame," one of the voices said.

"What happened to him?" said the other.

"From what I could find out, he's been in here for over a month. They found him beaten and bleeding to death along with his wife, I think."

"Oh no, who could be so cruel?"

"The police have no clue so far."

"He's been here a month, and they still don't know what happened to him?"

"Things work slowly in Daytona Beach."

"If he's in a coma, why are his eyes open?"

"That's how it is sometimes, their eyes are open but they can't see you," she explained. "I know this is your first time with a coma patient, unfortunately, it probably will not be your last,"

I could see the corners of faces as we passed other patients in the hall. Doctors and nurses scurried around amidst the constant chatter of the intercom. As I could see only above me and some of the fringe areas of my left and right, my view was mostly fixed on what I soon learned were two attractive young nurses. Also within my view was a bag of fluid towered over me, hanging off to my left with a tube dangling from it. *It was an IV,* I thought. They continued to navigate through the chaotic hallways, wheeling at a steady pace, occasionally shouting, "Coming through." Not knowing for sure what was real and what was not, I realized we were now on an elevator. The red head said to the other, "So what happened to his wife, is she here?"

I felt that familiar feeling of wanton anxiety. Holding with silent terror, I braced myself for her response.

"I'm not sure," she responded. "There were rumors that she was in the psych ward. Poor girl, she hasn't spoken a word since they found them."

"I wonder what could have been so awful?"

"I don't know, but it had to be terrible to do that to her."

For an entire month I would lay trapped in a complete coma, unable to tell my story and name my tormentors. The memories crept over me as I thought about Christy. I wondered if she even knew I was still alive. The elevator stopped, and as the doors pulled away from each other, they wheeled me off and down the hall. The hallway was very quiet, and the air was stiff and cold.

"This gives me the creeps," said the red headed nurse.

"Get use to it," said the other, "This is where they put all of the terminal and sleepers."

"Sleepers?"

"The comatose!"

"Why is it so cold?"

"Because the morgue is on this floor."

"You mean they put these patients right next to the morgue?"

"Yes, it's either a very bad joke or someone wants to help these people into their graves. Anyway, I just work here, I don't make policy. Come on— give me a hand so we can get the heck out of here."

"But what about him? Are we going to just leave him here?"

"This is his new home. He'll be here until he either dies or wakes up, which ever comes first."

"I don't feel good about this, Jan. Are you sure he'll be taken care of, I mean, all the way down here and all?"

"Not our problem any more kid. Loosen the straps and let's get out of here."

"I'm sorry, Mr. Broadhurste, I wish we didn't have to do this, but you'll be OK. I hope," said the red headed nurse.

"Well, what do you want to do Red take him home or what? Let's skedattle."

Red looked at me once more and whispered, "It will all be better soon."

She turned toward the door, and walked from my bed. It was so cold. Luckily Red had placed the sheet over my body and up to my chin. I wondered what she meant by, 'It will all be better soon'. *Did even she expect to see me soon dead?* It was so quiet. Up until now, the only thing that told me I was alive had been the sounds around me and occasional blurred faces. It was dark and cold. I couldn't move, I couldn't speak, and couldn't hear a thing. *How could these people be so insensitive? How could they just leave me here with the dead, and those expected to be dead soon?* It seemed quite clear; they didn't expect me to make it. *Please, let it come quickly,* I thought. Death had seemed so greedy in the past. When I was growing up people died around us all the time. The streets of south central were not easily forgotten—shootings, knifings and worse. Most of the time it was quick, although there were times when death could be agonizingly slow. One such time will probably never leave my mind.

It happened when I was in my early teen years. A couple of neighborhood kids, Fat Tony and Little Rob, had broken into the stalled, boxed cars on the railroad tracks. Breaking off the pad lock, they slid open the great wooden door. Inside they found an armed guard waiting with his weapon drawn. Quickly ducking under the rail car, they ran like the wind. The guard gave chase, and was closing in on them fast. Splitting up, Fat Tony ran up and over a hill toward the power shack, while Little Rob headed for the street. By the time the officer caught up to Little Rob, it was too late. The officer would find Rob's frame perilously dangling within a web of live wires. During the chase, Little

Rob tripped and fell off the edge of a stone cliff, landing smack in the middle of an entanglement of electrical wires that lay below. Every thirty seconds or so he would cry out in excruciating pain, begging to be rescued. It seemed the electricity would surge back and forth from one pole to another, in some attempt to reset itself with poor Little Rob right in the middle.

Meanwhile, the growing crowd gathered around, while the rescue team made efforts to shut off the power. Although I was quite young, I was struck by how many men were crying as if he were their son. There was plenty of misery to go around that day. On the next surge, we watched as his body twitched and pulled in all directions, his voice growing faint. Smoke oozed from his sneakers and his flesh was shriveled and horribly charred. "Please God somebody help me, I won't do it again. Please make it stop, it hurts so badly," he pleaded. Screams of horror erupted from the crowd. At that moment, I felt that a tiny piece of me had died; that things would never be the same. I didn't know it at the time, but I was witnessing the greed of death as it slowly plucked at this kid's body. Reinforcing its might, death showed itself to all of the onlookers. Little Rob died an unmerciful death, one excruciating moment at a time.

Many years later, I find myself living Little Rob's death. I know now how it feels to die a slow and agonizing death. It seems that not only is death greedy, it also has the audacity to be quite patient. I wondered if death was playing a game with me. I've heard people say the only thing worst than death itself, was waiting in anticipation for it to come. *I suppose I've always agreed in theory, but now I know this statement to be true,* I thought. I soon learned that it was the threat of death and its stench that could hold a person completely riddled with fear. Little Rob was without doubt, beside himself with fear, so too was I. At that moment, I felt closer to him than anyone else in the world. If death was playing a game with me, it wasn't hard to tell who was winning. *I don't know if you can cheat death, the best I could ask for I suppose would be to delay the taking. What an insidious thing it is when you can't even coax death into doing its duty,* I thought. *Surprisingly, I used to boldly tout that one cannot die until he gave in and accepted death. I couldn't have been more wrong. I soon learned that a truer statement would be that one cannot die until death decides to take you.* I was terrified as I fathomed the thought that death may actually have discriminating taste. It seemed that while nothing in life was certain, nothing in death was certain either. *Who would have thought that I would pray for death just as feverishly as I'd prayed for life?*

Something has to happen soon, I thought. I was going completely out of my mind. In fact, it felt as if I had long since been separated from my senses. The continual images that appeared in my head were all but unintelligible. *If only it wasn't so damned quiet,* I thought. *If only it wasn't so damned cold. If only it wasn't so dark and lonely.* Waiting to die proved to be the most crippling thing that my spirit has had to endure. My prayers seemed to have fallen on deaf ears. My suffering continued and my body steadily deteriorated. With my personhood gone, all that I had left was a shell of skin and bones. I couldn't see myself. I couldn't even feel myself. I could only hear myself think and I suppose that's something to be thankful for, but thanks for anything was beyond me at that point.

My dear father in heaven why have thou forsaken me? What have I done that has made me deserving of such punishment? What sins have I committed that would bring such continued wrath? I searched my mind and heart, but found no answers. I'd not been perfect, but I'd not been so evil that such perils would befall me. *Please God, help me to understand.*

Drifting in and out of sleep, I would awake from nightmares screaming to the fullest capacity of my voice, but no sound registered. I knew that I was screaming at times but I couldn't feel my mouth open. When last I slept, I dreamt that I was in a room much like my bedroom at home when I was a child. I was about ten years old and confined to my bed. It was pleasant enough with stuffed animals around and paper airplanes dangling from strings tacked to the ceiling. A crowded bookcase was built into the headboard of my bed and the sheets were covered with familiar cartoon characters. It was a fairly tidy room for a ten year old with a few toy soldiers scattered across the floor. It wasn't clear why I was confined to my bed but I was in my pajamas and was fairly playful as a normal ten year old would be. I was examining a model car that I had put together earlier when someone walked into the room. It was a woman with a familiar face, but not the face of my mother. She was there to give me some medication. I put up a fight about taking the medication, and was consequently threatened with punishment. With the resolve of a stubborn ten year old, I vowed not to take that, 'nasty stuff.' The woman called to someone outside the room and in came a doctor or at least someone in a white lab coat. With the voice of reason, the man bent over to explain to me the virtues of being a good little boy, when suddenly he turned quite stern. His stiff admonishing turned violent and his face grew twisted and grotesque. As he leaned over the bed, his legs grew in size and resembled the hind legs of a giant creature from some Greek mythological tale. His large and grossly distorted frame towered over my bed, as he lunged out with huge claw-like hands. With my throat firmly gripped in one of his huge claws, he pulled me closer lifting my body clear off the bed. Then he growled, "You dare to question my judgment?" Terrified beyond words, I looked toward the direction of the woman for safety. Her face was even more monstrous and contorted. Her eyes were filled with evil. She promised to give my bed and room to a more deserving kid. She spat in my face. She barked her words through big yellow teeth. Squirming with fright, I screamed a blood curdling scream which only seemed to excite them more.

In a flash, I sprang awake and for a moment felt relief. My lifeless body quickly reminded me that as bad as the dream was, it was only a temporary distraction, a temporary relief. The one good thing about nightmares is that they end. What was happening to me at that moment didn't seem to have an ending. It just continued to spiral downward into the depths of the unimaginable. The dreams continued and so did my torment. It felt like an eternity since they'd brought me down here, yet I'd not seen a soul. Sleep continued to overtake me, so I loosened my thoughts and gave in to the needed slumber.

More time had passed, and my hell had no less fury. I was still locked away in madness and I couldn't find my way out. It was still cold and still quiet. I thought I heard footsteps. I fought wildly to say something or move something, but I got no response. I felt my lips trying to part, but it just wasn't enough. Tears began to swell at the corners of my eyes, breaking free from the outer edges, streaming down the sides of my face. I hoped they would see the tears, and know that I was still alive. As the footsteps grew closer, I could also here the smooth sound of rubber wheels as they made their way across the floor. *Could it be that I was to receive a roommate?* Abruptly, the wheels stopped and the clang of a latch echoed through the hallway. I heard the sound of a heavy door opening. Much like the sound of a door on a meat locker, it swished with a gush of cold wind as if it were in a vacuum. The 'Morgue!' *Some fortunate soul is being laid to rest in a proper manner,* I thought. The smell and feel of death was all around me and I could swear that I felt it gently stroke my face, as if it were flirting with me. How absolutely wicked this thing is we call death. It shows more of itself every day. Not knowing if I was still awake or dreaming again, I felt my bed move. Directly above me shined a thin stream of bright light that penetrated deep into my eyes. The stream of light moved quickly from left to right and then it went away. I then heard the clicking of what sounded like a recorder and then he began to speak.

"This is Doctor Michaels in pre-morgue 5, the patient tagged Mr. Broadhurste shows no signs of life. He is a black male approximately six foot two inches, weighing, lets see here... oh God, that stinks; weighing approximately one hundred thirty pounds."

The lights were now on and it was clear that this doctor was examining me.

"As indicated on his chart, there are multiple contusions on the head and neck and multiple lacerations on the face. Removing the top sheet, the patient appears to be severely undernourished, no pulse is evident. Additional lacerations and scar tissue from emergency surgery approximately thirty days ago are evident. Wounds had not healed properly. Now turning the body over. My God! The body has been lying in its own waste for what I estimate to be a week or more. The underside of the body is leaking of blood and puss from multiple wounds that did not heal. Making a small incision on the back of the right thigh, oh shit," He remarked with disgust.

I felt nothing. I did however get a better look at the room. It was huge and there were many other beds seemingly occupied, but no one ever made a sound. Nothing!

The preliminary autopsy continued.

"The thigh, buttocks and rectal cavity are filled with maggots. Evidence of gangrene and the size of several round worms suggest deep flesh infestation. Scheduling a full open cavity exam set for tomorrow at nine am."

Turning my body flat on my back, hc then put a little salve on his upper lip, just as I had seen coroners do in the movies. All of the evidence was pointing to my being dead. I was cold, I couldn't move and my body smelled so bad that the doctor almost gagged twice. The handwriting was plainly written on the wall and all I had to do was read it. Dr.

Michaels pulled out a card from his top pocket. Quickly, he began to scribble something on it. Almost in one motion, he then began to remove the needle from my arm, along with the bag of liquid over my head. After tossing the two items into the trash, he walked to the far end of the bed. In total disbelief, I could faintly feel what he was doing. Dr. Michaels was putting a toe tag around my big toe. My insides felt as if they had been smashed into a thousand pieces, and the realization of his actions hit like a Mack truck. Soon, I was in motion— on my way to the meat locker— on my way to the morgue. I knew then if I wasn't dead, I would soon be. Nothing living that I knew of could survive such frigid temperatures for long. Reeling with anguish and exhausted fear, I resolved to get his attention somehow. Crying dry tears and screaming at the top of my lungs, which no one heard, I concentrated with all that I had left to move something, anything. It was no use. I just couldn't do it. Suddenly, I could feel my eyes blink, and I knew it was real. I could actually feel something besides my tears. It was the first time I was able to cover my exposed pupils since I'd been down here. The warmth of the inner lining of my eyelids bathed my eyes with salty liquid and the dull pain was heartily welcomed. I could feel again. In a panic, I blinked as hard and as often as I could. I was still moving closer and closer to the morgue and he was not paying any particular attention to me at all. Over the intercom rang, "Paging Dr. Michaels, code blue in ICU 4." He paused for a moment, checked his pager, and started wheeling me again in the direction of the morgue. In a rush, he dropped his clipboard and a pocket full of pens, just as he was reaching out for the latch on the giant door. As he bent down to pick up his things, I heard the light echoing of what sounded like a woman's heels.

"Dr. Michaels," she called, "We've been looking all over for you. You have an emergency. It's Mrs. Miller. She's in."

"Yes, I know— ICU 4. Thank you."

"Where are you taking Mr. Broadhurste?" she asked.

"You knew this guy?" he responded.

"Well, no, but I helped to bring him down. Is he going to make it?"

"I'm afraid he's expired. Can you do me a favor?"

As he was running down the hall he asked her to wheel me into the morgue. She was quite squeamish about it as she tried calling back to him.

"You sure this can't......wait?"

He was gone. It was all up to her now. *Would she be the one to seal my fate? Who knew?* She walked around the gurney, and reached out for the latch on the door. Abruptly, she pulled away, seemingly startled by the frost on the handle. Standing back against the wall, staring straight at the large door, she took a deep breath and mumbled something to herself. As she passed within my view on her way back for her second attempt, I caught a full look at her. It was Red! Feeling a twinge of excitement, I tried again to move my eyes. Exhausted from the last try, I knew it would be difficult. "There," she said, "it's open. Now all I have to do is go in."

With the great door open, and the icy fog billowing from inside, she stood petrified. She caught her breath, and stepped back from the door. Shaking her head as if to snap out of it, she came over to me. "You may be gone," she said, "But I can pretend this story has a happy ending. Even it's only for a moment." Then, just like before, she reached down and began to pull the sheet up and over my chest. Again, the moment of truth was at hand. With all the strength that I could muster, I concentrated all of my energy on urging my eye lids to move. In the meantime, she was still lovingly tucking the sheet around my body. Miraculously, I felt my eyelids begin to flutter. I blinked once, and then again. Every time I blinked it became easier. As I focused on the once flushed face of this angel, I knew she had to have seen my eyes move. Her face was now white as a sheet. I could see her body, stiff at first, now swaying ever so slightly. Blinking even stronger now, I looked deep into her eyes, searching for compassion. Just then she let out a scream, loud and full like I had never heard anyone scream before. She dropped her chart, pushed the gurney away from her, and with the morgue door flung wide open, she bolted down the hall, screaming and calling for help. Scurrying like a scared rabbit, she stumbled and hobbled her way back to the elevator.

Somehow she had stepped in and gave me another shot at living. My God had not forsaken me after all. *Thank you Lord, thank you for another chance.*

Chapter 3

"Redemption"

I had lain in the hallway for perhaps thirty minutes feeling quite excited and anxious. I tried to remain calm while anticipating the redemption committee. With relief in sight, finally my mind turned inward and gave in to a rich but temporary slumber. I dreamed again of dragons and jackals and two headed monsters. Suddenly, my dreams were interrupted by the thunderous harangue of voices and the high pitched screech of squeaky wheels.

"There he is doctor. I know he's still alive. He looked right through me and even blinked a few times," exclaimed Red.

In a frenzy, the team of people began hooking up tubes to my arms and hanging bags of plasma above my head. Running along side the speeding gurney a technician shouted, "Got a pulse, but very weak blood pressure."

"Clear the way, coming through," another shouted.

The shot they gave me must have been to put me to sleep. I tried to enjoy my redemption, but I felt as if I was going to sleep right through it. The commotion was still fairly active, but the sound was growing dim. The lights and faces began to disappear, and finally everything turned to black. Unable to fight it, I drifted into a tight, sound sleep.

Sometime later, I awoke to the crackling chatter of pages going out over the intercom. In my face was the familiar thin stream of light coming from what seemed like a small pen light. I was being examined by the chief resident and a half dozen first year residents. I overheard them talk of the emergency surgery, and how close I had come to death. Noting the large number of lacerations and contusions, one of the residents asked just how I ended up here. The chief resident answered, "No one knows what really happened. Maybe when Mr. Broadhurste gains his strength we can all put this little mystery to rest." He then reached up, grabbed the top end of the large curtain, and drew it the full way around my bed. I could hear him place the chart back on the wall and the sound of footsteps disappeared into the hallway.

The door closed and then opened again. The footsteps told me the person was coming my way. The curtains were drawn back gently, revealing a bright, warm smile and fiery red hair.

"Good morning Mr. Broadhurste, so glad you could be with us this fine morning."

It was Red.

I thought, *She's quite chipper.* She saved my life, but having to sit through her perky monologue was still an adjustment. She talked about everything; including her aunt Mabel, the one with the six hairs growing out of two great big old warts on her neck. She talked incessantly, as she carefully changed my dressings and reconnected a fresh feeding tube. Pausing for a moment, she asked, "Am I talking too much? Because if I am you know I'll just stop." Looking down at me she said, "OK, how about if we try to communicate with each other? I know you can blink your eyes, so why don't we start there. If you can understand me blink your eyes once."

With considerable ease, I blinked my eyes shut, paused and then opened them.

"Wonderful," she said with excitement. "Now, one blink will stand for yes and two blinks will stand for no, do you understand?"

I blinked once, and she was very pleased.

"Are you in pain?" she asked.

I blinked twice.

She replied, "Good, at least for now. Eventually, you will begin to feel pain. That, believe it or not, will be a good sign."

She said I was recovering rather well, but it would be a while before I would be considered out of danger.

"We have the best doctors here, and I'm confident that they will take great care of you. By the way, I'm Nurse Helen Tate, and I'll be looking in on you from time to time."

It was so comforting to know that someone was actually acknowledging me as a person. My body still breathed life, and my mind still sought the warm embrace of understanding and acknowledgement. *So sweet, was this creature to bring hope back to my hollowed out shell.* As she gave me a sponge bath, she took great care lifting my lifeless arms to wash their pits. She then bent them at the elbow once, then twice in an effort to increase circulation. All the while, she still talked about her family. Finally, she stopped and asked, "Is this boring you to tears, or what?" As she moved forward to read my response, I again closed my eyes and then opened them, and then after a slight pause, I blinked once again, answering no— I was not bored to tears. I tried to smile, but I didn't know if she could see it. "Nice to see you have a sense of humor, and thank you for that answer," she replied with a chuckle. She finished my arms and down my chest. I couldn't feel much of what was happening. Occasionally I would feel remote twinges of pain depending on how much Nurse Helen manipulated my limbs. As she got around to my genital area, for the first time I felt embarrassed by her presence. She fumbled around with the dressings a bit more when suddenly she shot a look back at me. Our eyes met. Now that I had pretty good control of my eyes, the most I could do was to try and speak through their expressions. With them I told her of my embarrassment. I looked down, as my back was propped up slightly, then back at her and then finally, I closed my eyes to seal the deal. With sincere concern she called for me to open my eyes. I opened them.

"I can only imagine how awful all this must be for you. I promise you, there is nothing to be ashamed about. I am a qualified, registered nurse and you are a patient in need of my care. If it's alright, I would like to finish you up so you can get some rest. Will that be alright Mr. Broadhurste? Blink once if yes," she added. Blinking once, I told her to continue. She finished the sponge bath, changed my IV, and pulled the sheets up to my chest and over my bare arms.

"Sweet dreams, Mr. Broadhurste, and welcome back to the living," she said with genuine kindness. I found that I did indeed dream sweet dreams that night.

The following morning I awoke to the sweet aroma of fresh flowers and a hint of pine, presumably from a floor cleaner. The room was full of light, although the shades were partially drawn. I could see the flowers on the far end of the counter, even though they were on the other side of the room. Without even realizing it, I had looked from one side of the room to the other. Ordinarily, this would be a rudimentary chore. But this time, I was able to see each side of the room because I had actually moved my head from one side to the other. Shocked to tears, I began to move my neck even more. Up and down, and side to side, I moved my neck with relative ease. Happy beyond words, I tried to mouth the words thank you, and miraculously enough, I could feel my mouth begin to form the words. Nothing came out but I did feel my face move. Hardly able to contain my excitement, I touched my lip with the tip of my tongue. *When you lose absolutely everything*, I thought, *small victories are the only things keeping you alive*. It was so gratifying to know that I still had lips and a tongue. I could actually begin to sense how long it had been since my mouth and tongue were last in use. It's very difficult to describe the feeling of rebirth. With pasty mouth and throat I'm now able to feel my vocal cords, and hope to be able to speak soon. I was sure that I, as a person, had ceased to exist. I felt like death warmed-over; like everyone knew I was dead, but me. The corpse it seemed had begun to resemble a living human being again....

Chapter 4

"Remembering Christine"

Two weeks later!

It was seven a.m., time for my morning wash. The sun was shining brightly and the birds were singing, seemingly without a care in the world. My therapy was going well, although it consisted mainly of bed exercises. My voice returned and I'd regained use of my arms. The doctors prescribed a cocktail of antibiotics and my chart suggested that my paralysis should be temporary. In strutted Red—bright and energetic as ever, wearing a warm smile and a blue knitted shawl draped across the padded shoulders of her white uniform.

"Top of the morning to ya Mr. Broadhurste."

Top of the morning to you too, I replied.

"I trust you're up for your morning bath," she said, grinning and giggling shyly into her open palms. Placing a colorful bouquet of flowers into a vase, and then filling it with water, she added, "I thought these would help brighten the room for you."

Thank you, but I see that you're never going to let me live this thing down, are you? I asked.

"Not as long as you keep 'rising' to the occasion," she retorted.

With that she burst into uncontrolled laughter while prepping me for my bath. I was a little embarrassed, but I also enjoyed her laughter and the sponge baths as well. Since I'd begun to regain feeling throughout my limbs, I had also begun to regain a great deal of feeling in other areas. Couple those feeling with the warm and rhythmic touch of a rather buxom young nurse and a sponge bath would begin to take on a brand new meaning. Well, needless to say for the last several days I've found it extremely difficult if not impossible to refrain from becoming quite aroused. It would happen less than a quarter of the way through my bath. She would sponge my entire body with loving hands, taking special care not to miss an inch. Under my arms and over my shoulders, gently she caressed my skin. From time to time she'd leave the sponge in the bowl and wash my body with her hands. She'd lay me down and turn me on my side, working her way from back to front, her fiery red hair gently brushed across my face bringing with it a soft hint of jasmine. Not saying a word she worked her way down, across my chest and on to my groin area. By then I'd be fully erect. As if this was perfectly natural she sponged all around my awakened manhood as if it were a newly potted plant that just needed the surrounding soil to be tended to. I would apologize profusely, but she'd simply say it was all part of the job, that if I enjoyed it, to consider it an added bonus.

I was happy to know that she had such a matter of fact attitude about this, particularly because I was most aroused from thoughts of my wife, Christine. I'd think of how her shapely breasts would bounce about in cadence with every youthful step. Her curves were like that of a Greek goddess, supple and sweet; skin, smooth as silk. Her eyes were dark but cheerful and warm. These images were the ones that took me away, the ones that lined my thoughts just long enough to mask some of the pain. And for brief moments of 'suspended disbelief' I'd be able to escape to a world where no one else existed except Christine and me. Feeling a little light headed, I slowly drifted out of consciousness. There, I'd lay dazed. Drifting in and out of awareness, I began to think back to how I ended up here. My mind began to run foggy clips of emergency room images, sprinkled with startling sounds of doom. A prevailing sense of panic overtook me as I broke into a cold sweat. In my mind, I saw the perfectly manicured lawn of what must have been the hospital. The spinning red and white lights would intermittently illuminate the faces of the white cotton clad workers as they busily scurried about. Sights, sounds and shouts. The images were stronger now, as they began to remind me of darker days, the likes of which even my nightmares were afraid. As I lay, the memory of my torment began to play itself out. Yet again with no mercy, it clutched me tightly to its foul bosom. Never to escape its grasp, I sat and watched as it tore out my insides, reinforcing the knowledge that no changes were allowed. Without my permission and before my very eyes, the true nightmares of the past began again. And with that came a flood of left over emotions that poured out onto the floor and all over the room. My grief filled the air with its poison, aggressively smothering the sunshine that peeked its way through the blinds. The smell of the freshly cut flowers seemed to bring thoughts of death and isolation. On the verge of a nervous break down, I hastened to constrain my emotions, when I felt the kindness of a warm hand gently wipe the tears from my face. I looked up and it was Red. Seeing that I was obviously shaken, she pulled me close. Helping to purge myself of this God awful pain, she held me tight promising that every thing would be alright. In her arms, I curled and cried like a baby. The more I tried to stop, the less control I had. Whimpering like a lost child, I told her about the abduction. How they utterly destroyed my life. How they took Christine away from me and did these terrible things to her. I told her what they did to me, how ashamed I was. How one day I'd have my revenge. My grief began to subside and soon I felt numb all over. Thoughts of Christine's whereabouts filled my head. *Was she even still alive?* I wondered. Of that, I had no clue. *Was there anything to the rumors that she was in a mental ward? If that is true even, what ward? What hospital?* I questioned.

Sensing my quiet distance Red asked, "Thinking about your wife, a?"

Yes, I replied.

"Would you like me to ask around? This is a hospital you know and people love to gossip."

Yes, I said, *yes I'd like that very much, thank you.*

With that she wiped the running mascara from her face, as her eyes had swelled with liquid, then straightened the collar of her white blouse.

"Good thing no one walked in on us," she joked, "they might have gotten the wrong idea."

You think? I asked.

"Absolutely," she said.

With a shy girlish grin, she buttoned the top two buttons of her blouse. "Absolutely," she repeated under her breath. By then it was close to nine AM., time for my therapy. Excited about the prospects of finding my wife, I began to rattle on about how we met and how we shared everything. How we had not been married a year yet and our plans of starting a family. *We were both eager to start a family because neither of us had any. That was what first attracted us to one another, beyond the physical. We each understood the life long pain of the other. Abandoned by our natural parents and sometimes abused while in foster care, we would each dream of the other and not even know it. Longing for a soul mate, I drifted in and out of relationships in hopes of finding peace; the peace that I could not find alone. Frustrated and hardened from failed relationships, I decided to concentrate most on my studies and began to stick my nose deep into my many text books. Closing inward, I would routinely stay at the library until it closed. So much so that the head librarian asked me if I'd like to work there, since I closed the place most nights anyhow, that I may as well get paid for it. This was the perfect job for me, so I took it. Fortunately, I was in school on a full scholarship and didn't really need the money but this job would at least help me get a few extra small creature comforts. It was there one night that I began to see this vision of pure loveliness.*

Every night for a week I'd see her and each time I convinced myself that this night was somehow just not the right night to approach her. Finally one night after dinner, I told myself that I would do it, that I'd just strut up to her and 'tell her like it is.' Yeah sure I would, but I decided to try anyway. With the awkwardness of a kid trying to walk in his fathers work boots, I walked up to her table and asked if she needed any help. She looked around, shrugged and asked what kind of help did I mean? Feeling as if I'd just bitten off more than I'd ever be able to chew, I began to walk away backwards, apologizing again and again as if I was a peasant who had just disturbed the princess. Overtaken by the sexiest smile that was ever aimed in my direction, I stopped in my tracks. "It surely has taken you a long time to finally say something to me," she said. "I thought maybe you didn't like girls who could read, not to mention those who could write too, because I can do both, you know."

With that, I was a goner—putty in her hands. From that day on we were inseparable. We ate lunch together most days and shared most of our evening hours together as well. We would always talk about living near a beach and living on a boat. We even talked about getting a mobile home and traveling the country. We were hopeless romantics and fell deeper in love as we frequently talked of our future together. On schedule we both graduated last June and decided we'd buy that mobile home. Saying our last goodbye's to UCLA, we loaded up the camper and set our sights on Las Vegas. There we were married. We hung around for a few weeks before we made the final plan to drive as far east as possible. We wanted to see if the Atlantic was any different from the Pacific. It wasn't. The East however, did give us the best vantage point for watching the sun rise, of which we did often. We'd make love on barren beaches near the rocks. Beginning with the glow of the moon and ending with the rising of the sun; bringing with it a glorious new day with all the wonderment of new beginnings. Wide eyed and idealistic, we faced the world together and nothing could tear us apart. Nothing; until that day, the ugliest day of my life. The day I prayed for death and no one heard my cry. When my cries were heard, it was too late. My once vibrant spirit was now dead and buried, as I'd lost the comfort of our intertwined souls. That was our first day in Daytona Beach.

Tired from the long drive, we stopped at a clearing in a wooded area where we planned to stay the night. I pulled down the shades and drew all of the curtains closed, locked the front door and checked the rear hatch to be sure that it was also locked. We got undressed and snuggled up tight as we prepared to sleep off our complete exhaustion. With Christine totally wiped out, I awoke to the sound of escaping air, as I watched the camper begin to tilt inward to its left side. From the rear of the camper, I could see that the front was decidedly higher than the back. Dreading the idea of having to fix a flat, I dismissed the sound and closed my eyes. Suddenly, I could hear the other rear tire squealing from escaping air. I looked down at Christine, by now she was balled in a tight fetal position. Not having the heart to wake her, I put on some pants and grabbed my boots and a flashlight. I went out and around the front of the camper, down to the back then I stopped. I bent down to take a better look and I saw that the tire had been slashed. Panic stricken, I threw myself up against the side of the camper and turned off my flashlight. Then from inside the camper came a flash of light. It moved quickly from the front to the rear and then it stopped. The light went off then popped back on. Shining brightly on a bearded toothless face, the light implanted a horror that left me petrified. I began to bang on the side of the camper, 'Christine wake up, wake up.' Making my way around the side of the camper, I ran hard towards the opened door. Before I could make it, I was struck hard over the head from behind. As I tried to get to my feet, I had the wind kicked out of me with a steel tipped biker's boot. Out of the corner of my eye, I could see Christine struggling to free herself from the grip of this toothless ape. I looked up for the last time to see Christine running for the highway. Just then one of the bastards spit a large wad of tobacco filled saliva in my face followed by the bottom of his boot. That was when my lights went out. When I awoke, I was chained to that old *tree stump and you know the rest. For that, my life will never be the same.*

I looked up and again Red was in tears. Again, her mascara was badly running down her face. She swore she'd help in any way she could to find Christine. I took her at her word. With that she said she needed to go to her locker and that she'd look in on me before her mid afternoon break. Soon after therapy, I ate lunch and fell into a deep sleep.

Later on that day about three o'clock or so, I was snatched from my slumber. In burst Red. Shouting whispers she called, "Mr. Broadhurste, Mr. Broadhurste, wake up, wake up." She told me of how she asked all of the nurses on her shift about me and my case and that none of them knew just what happened to her.

I said *that's not exactly good news.*

"Well of course not," she retorted. "But what is good is that I was thumbing through some old files in the hospital's media center, you know they keep all types of old records and such; well anyway," she said, "I came across the file of a 'Jane Doe' that fit the description of your wife."

Are you sure? I asked. *Did it really match, and in this hospital? What made it a match anyway? Did you get a copy?* I asked.

"Slow down," she said, "I wasn't able to get a copy and I wasn't able to get the whole file."

Well, why not? I asked.

"Because the files that I discovered were only cataloging files."

What do you mean, cataloging files? I asked.

"I wondered about that too, it doesn't match up with any of the standard logs that I know of," she responded.

You mean she's been cataloged like some junk yard part in a warehouse somewhere?

"Perhaps we shouldn't jump to conclusions; I may have misunderstood Dr. Michaels' terminology. Anyway, the entire file should be somewhere on disk, probably in my boss's office, and that's somewhere that I just can't go. At least not without his authorization," she added.

Why not? I demanded.

"Because, in the first place, if I got caught I'd be fired! And if that's not a good enough reason, I wouldn't even know how to operate his computer, I was never exactly computer literate, you know what I mean?"

No problem, I said, take me with you. You could be the look out and I could search the files.

"I'm sorry Mr. Broadhurste, but that's just out of the question, we'd better come up with a better plan. I just thought I'd share that bit of news, I hope it helps, now try to get some rest and I'll see you tomorrow, so long."

With that, she was off.

Tossing and turning, I was unable to get any real sleep, and ended up pacing the floor throughout the night. While formulating a plan to get to those computer files, I felt my insides turn to jelly. *Could it really be true, could Christine still be alive and maybe even still, in this hospital?* I wondered. Convincing myself to take Red's advice, I decided not to jump to conclusions. I thought it best to first devise a plan to get a good look at those files. Fatigued and overburdened with worry, I took my medication and prepared myself for bed. As I lay there, I thought of what I would say to her if I were to find her again. *Would she recognize me? Or would my face be just another among many strange faces?* Bending Red's rule, I fantasized of a joyous reunion with Christine, while steadily trying to prepare myself for the inevitable dead end. With my mind reeling with thoughts of Christine, I shut my eyes and waited for nice dreams to come to my rescue. Just as I was all but firmly seated on the wings of a glorious dream, I heard a commotion in the hallway. The sound was faint but it definitely broke the silence. I rushed to my feet and grabbed the robe at the foot of the bed. With bare feet, I quietly made my way over to the door. The sound was getting louder. There seemed to be mumbling of some kind. I couldn't make it out but it did sound human at least. The sound was headed straight for my door and soon I felt the under-swell of a growing panic. I jumped back away from the door and picked up the water pail, ready to hammer any thing that walked through that door, I was terrified. The strange commotion passed right by my door until the sound drifted to the farthest end of the hall. *I don't dare open the door,* I thought, *besides that pail was not much of a weapon any way.* I thought about it again and decided that I would take a peek through a partially cracked door. I slightly cracked the door and peered out into the hallway. There I saw a parade of hooded figures as they took their leave through the stairwell at the end of the hall. My eyes panned from left to right trying to take in all that I could. Widening the crack in the door for a better look, the door hinge suddenly let out a squeal. At that one of the figures stopped and looked directly at my door. Motioning my way, the dark hooded figure started in my direction. Quickly, but quietly I pushed the door shut. Racing back to my bed, I placed my slippers side by side at the foot of the bed, quickly slipping under the covers. There I lay as still as could be, holding my breath even to avoid moving an inch. Listening intensely, I waited. Then suddenly, I began to hear that familiar whining sound. It was the door. Someone or something was opening my door. Still as a corpse, I lay motionless. And like the prey being surveyed by the predator, I felt the stare of iced cold eyes as they invaded my petrified body. I didn't dare move a muscle— not an eyelash. The door soon eased shut and the sound of the figure grew farther and farther from my door. I didn't quite know why I was so frightened but something about those figures seemed cold and less than human. Needless to say, I didn't get any sleep that night and none the next. Again, I heard the familiar commotion but didn't dare go near my door. And again, I'd lie still until the sound was no more....

Chapter 5

"Nathaniel"

Another week had gone by and I'd been up on my feet quite a bit. I began to walk around the hospital at night, sometimes for the exercise, but mostly out of sheer boredom. I'd make believe that I couldn't walk too well, just so no one would suspect me of walking the grounds. Actually, I could walk rather well and could probably run if I had to. I would fake my paralysis also to spite my night nurse who would at times take away my wheel chair because I hadn't eaten dinner. I never understood why, but she was unusually aggressive and mean spirited. It had gotten to the point that I was sure not to finish my meal, just so I could freely walk the grounds.

The lighting in the hallways was surprisingly dim, particularly at night. According to Red, there had been many cut backs at the hospital as such they would turn on only one of the three panels of lights for each floor during night shift hours. The hallways themselves were long and drab, with vaulted ceilings and greenish colored paint that was badly bubbling and cracking along the base boards. The doors were white and the floors were heavily scuffed in spots but well polished and waxed in others. The stale air swelled with the strong smell of alcohol and cleaning solvents. Increasingly sullen but bored non- the-less, I began to rummage through anything unlocked. Supply closets and linen rooms were fair game and even the rooms of other patients. I even discovered the office of one Dr. W.H. Michaels, Red's boss. Curiously enough the floors leading into his office bore the heaviest scuff marks. Of course the door was always locked. I'd soon be able to hatch a plan to check on Dr. Michaels' files as soon as I was able to convince Red that something bad was going on. I was sure that soon enough, I'd have the evidence that I needed to persuade her.

Just last night while on my usual rounds about two Am., I heard a steady commotion clamoring its way up the stairs. In a panic, I frantically grabbed at every door in sight. Trapped between the elevators and this increasingly loud commotion, I raced for cover. Still lunging from door to door, one locked after another, the commotion began to close in. Now having reached the farthest end of the hall I came to a door marked exit. A small glassed porthole in the door gave clearance to the steps that lay on the other side. I hurriedly clawed the door in an effort to twist its knob to freedom. Feverishly, I tugged and twisted but to no end, the door was locked from the other side and its steel was not going to give way to my weak shoulder. Cornered and trapped like an animal, I thrashed about, as if looking for a weakness in a cage. With my back to the wall and my eyes firmly affixed on the exit door at the far end of the hall, I waited impatiently for my open discovery. Oddly enough, I soon became quite calm. I began to ready myself for defeat and hoped that I could take whatever punishment dealt me. With nerves exploding inside like fire works, I heard the swing action of a slide bolt ring out into the hallway. Simultaneously, I caught a glimpse of a tiny dark figure out of the corner of my eye, as it darted down the stairs. In a split second my brain screamed to me, *Try the door, try the door.* As the rusty sounding door began to open at the end of the hall, I reached down, twisted the knob and the door opened. Bursting with terror, I bolted to the other side. Slowly, I closed the door and quietly turned the little knob on the lock. Breathing a sigh of relief, I began to walk down the stairs somewhat dragging myself against the wall. I made it out of that close call but had no idea how. Terror would not soon lesson its grip on me. It would squeeze and squeeze until my insides felt as if they would explode with horrible anxiety. I thought, *I know where I am now, I know that I'm in hell.* I thought about many things that morning as I walked back to my room. I thought about who it was or what had unlocked that door. Not to mention what all of those hooded figures were and why they were so awkward and clumsy. I made it back down to my floor and into my room. Drenched with sweat, I wiped myself off and changed my tee shirt. I laid there thinking of how I needed to find Christine and get far away from that strange place. *This place was evil,* I thought. *This place has secrets that chill me to the bone.*

I just laid there in my bed, numb. Paralyzed with fright, I waited and prayed for sleep. With the hopes of escaping on the next irregularly scheduled dream, I stared at the ceiling above. Drifting deeper into the depths of despair, my mind began to close in on itself. Like a vault, the doors of my mind slammed shut, in the hopes of shutting out the absurd. It didn't work. Helplessly, I began to completely disassociate myself from my new reality.

The coarse and prickly nature of my memories tore at everything decent in me. They would leave a terrible trail of damage in their wake, whenever they decided to pay me a visit. Announced or unannounced they caused too much destruction and therefore had to be banished from my mind. Resting on the unsafe notion that I had shielded myself well, I covered myself with my blanket, tucking my face into the pillow. Already, my lockout was being tested as I heard a rumble in the closet. Feeling the pound in my chest grow stronger, I fixed my gaze upon the door. *There it is again, a shuffling sound, I was sure, there really is something in my closet,* I thought. Looking through the streams of dust filled light as it crept its way through the partially closed blinds, I surveyed the decorative spirals in the wood checking for even a glimmer of movement. As expected, it soon came. The brass knob began to turn and my heart was in my throat. The door began to open and so did my mouth as I let out a short but full yell. Falling off the bed and to the floor, I looked up to see a tiny hooded creature shooting out of the closet and into a corner around the farthest side of the bed. Shocked and deathly afraid, I jumped to my feet and then onto the counter. I grabbed whatever I could and began to pelt the position of this thing. This exact miniature replica of the things that I saw outside my door, jumped from the floor up onto the counter directly across from me. Completely covered with fabric, the form squatted in silence; looking it seemed, straight out at me. Unsure of exactly what to do, I slowly swung my legs around and off the top, down to the front of the ledge. Reaching out for my tray, I grabbed a piece of fruit from yesterdays' lunch. With an underhand motion, I tossed the fruit in its direction. Catching the fruit from the air, it immediately raised the peach to its mouth, devoured it in no time and then spit the hard seed to the floor. Surprised, but strangely pleased, I sat quietly and eagerly waited for something to happen. It was still quite dark in the room and the body of this thing was still very much obscured by both the dark and the robe that dwarfed it completely. In silence, I studied its small form. *Was it the result of some strange experiments that go on in this hospital?* I thought. *Is this thing human or is it some sort of primate, a chimpanzee perhaps?* My mind raced with wonderment and anticipation. I slipped off the ledge onto my feet and landed with a thump. The tiny hooded figure jumped back and onto its feet, standing firm on the ledge as if poised to leap. Realizing how aggressive my move must have been, I pushed forward my open palms and tried to reason with it. With the hopes that at some level this thing would understand, I began to speak to it. *What are you?* I asked, as I made my way around toward the door. *Who are you, do you understand me? I mean you no harm, do you understand?* No response! Having a clear shot for the door, I began to reassess my situation. *Do I make a B-line for the door and run for help or do I keep trying to communicate with this thing, whatever it is?*

I want to be your friend, I said, *but if you don't, I'm going right out that door.*

With that the dark figure jumped to the floor. *Oh God, I've scared it again,* I shouted aloud. In a panic, I stepped back against the door. It motioned toward me and I clinched my fists in preparation for the fight of my life. At that, it stopped in its tracks. Seemingly, it sensed my new hostility and began to slowly back away. Immediately, I unclenched my fists and said I was sorry, that I was just scared. What it did next astonished me to silence. Dragging a short dark train of fabric, it began to walk directly toward me. Raising its arms in the way that I had before, it continued to close. With its arms now completely outstretched, I began to see emerging from the edges of both sleeves, tiny dark hands. The hands were like that of a child, they were dark and seemingly aged, but one thing for sure, they were human.

Still unsure of exactly what was under that robe, I stood in silence. With my eyes firmly fixed on the hooded figure, it came within steps of me and began to raise its hands toward its hood. With both hands the hood was removed, revealing the somber and swollen face of a little boy. Completely astonished, I slid down to the floor. I couldn't believe my eyes. His face was badly bruised, yet his eyes were warm and cheerful. I didn't know what to think. In fact my mind was jumbled with all sorts of theories. When I finally got a hold of myself, I noticed the boy had completely removed his robe. Underneath he wore the clothes of the old share croppers, much like the ones the slaves wore in the movie, 'Roots'. His shirt was missing most of its buttons and was clasped together only by one. His little pants were rolled up at the bottoms and he wore a rope for a belt. The poor little guy had absolutely nothing on his feet, both of which were heavily scarred and swollen. It seemed that every exposed part of his body was covered with old cuts and new bruises.

What's your name, I asked.

No answer. Instead he went over to the small lamp on the end table and turned it on. With that, the light revealed the extensive damage that had been done to his little face and head, as well as his arms and legs. Then I asked again, *what is your name?* He looked up at me and seemed as if he was going to mouth his name, when instead he opened his mouth. Inside was a sight that almost made me throw up, his tongue was gone. Not just gone, but jaggedly removed as if it had been ripped out of his mouth. He stared down at me as I looked up at him. His expression told a horrible tale of pain and suffering. With eyes turning a deep red he looked at me with his head slightly turned to his left and mumbled what I made out to be "Why". "Why, why, why", he repeated over and over again. Bursting into tears, he collapsed. Falling forward, he landed squarely between my outstretched arms, plunging into my chest. As he moaned and wailed, I held him tightly. Clutching him close to me, he cried for more than an hour. Desperately, I tried to hold back my tears but it was too overwhelming, I was heart-broken. I had never seen a child suffer so. I tried to console him, but his pain and sadness were too great. There we sat on the floor, up against the door, where I was prepared to sit until this kid was ready to move.

Then without warning, he jumped to his feet and like a frighten deer, dashed for the closet. Not sure what was going on, I leaned forward to look in the direction of the closet, when I began to hear a familiar rustling sound outside my door. Immediately, I rushed for the lamp and turned it off. I heard the commotion getting louder and closer— with that, I ran for my bed and jumped in. While faking a deep sleep, I laid there waiting to see if my door would open, but it didn't. After fifteen minutes or so the muffled sounds stopped just as suddenly as they started. I sat there for a while wondering if I should look out into the hallway. I chose not to look. I waited some more. Soon after, the boy returned and I knew the coast was clear. It was he after all who heard the commotion long before I did. Again, I asked him his name. It was very difficult making it out at first, but I'm pretty sure that it's Nathaniel. He motioned with his right index finger and his left hand that he could write. He then asked if I had pencil and paper. I stood to open the blinds a bit, intending to use the light shining brightly from the glow of a full moon. We sat in the center of the room just inside of where the light fell onto the floor. Nathaniel, who looked to be no more than eight or nine, was quite smart and could write rather well, indeed for someone so young. Thus we began to communicate.

He told me that he was ten years old and that he had been in this hospital since they took his mother away.

Where did they take her? I asked.

He wrote, "She got sick one day so we came to the hospital. At first they said she would be ok then she got sicker. I went to ask the doctor about my mommy and he wasn't there, but when I got back to her room she was gone. I ran down the hall looking for her, but I didn't find her. Then I walked down a long hallway, I knew I was lost but I kept looking for my mommy. Then I saw a big door with a big window in it, when I looked through it I saw my mommy on a table. Her arm was hanging off the iron table and her eyes were open. I saw him. He was cutting parts off my mommy. He was talking into a tape recorder saying how much money he was going to get from my mommy's parts. I started to cry and he heard me. That's when he grabbed me, pulled me in and made me look at my mommy. Her whole middle was empty. All the stuff was gone and she didn't even look like mommy any more. Then he reached up on his tray and grabbed some kind of tool that looked like the pliers that my mommy kept in her car. Then he told me to open my mouth. I didn't so he choked me until I did. Then he reached in my mouth and pulled my tongue until it ripped in the middle. When I woke up I had stitches in my mouth and these clothes on. I never saw my mommy again. I was nine and a half when she died and now I'm ten. Ever since then I've lived here in the hospital, in the basement."

How can you live in the hospital for months and no one know?

He wrote, "I live in the basement with the others, when it's light outside, but when it's dark I sneak upstairs to the lunch room for food."

But how could you go so long without being caught? I asked.

"I can go anywhere in the hospital, through the vents," he wrote. With that he showed me a small hole that he had made in the closet which led to the main air-conditioning ducts.

Who are the others? I asked.

"I don't know," he mumbled, with a shrug.

He wrote that they were always coming and going, that they never stayed the same. He said he would see people for a few days, sometimes a few weeks, but never more than that.

In garbled tongue he said, "They looked mostly like you and me, but they always had something wrong with them."

What do you mean? I asked.

"They would always have to bring them up from the basement, mostly at night, mostly."

Do you know what they did to them then? I asked.

Continuing on he said, "The strong ones are fixed up. They get their teeth fixed and any cuts or anything, they fix up. The other ones, the sick ones like my mommy, had their parts cut out so the doctor could get money for them."

He also told me that on the first day there everyone gets their tongue's cut out, all except those who are being used as foreman or something.

I asked, *what did you mean by; they mostly looked like you and me?*

He responded in a high pitched but muffled voice, "They're all black, mostly."

Sitting there dumbfounded, I asked, *where do they take the people, you know the strong ones?*

"I don't know," he wrote. "They forgot about me so when they come to take the people away, I hide. When I come back they have new people, and I never see the others again."

Can you take me to where you live, I asked.

He wrote, "You're too big to fit through the hole."

Are the ducts big enough for me, I asked.

He wrote, "No, but the laundry chute is."

Where is that? I asked.

He held up one finger indicating that it was on the first floor. Pausing for a moment, I thought of how bizarre and unbelievable this was. But it was really happening right in front of my face. The boy was real and so was his pain. And his tongue had surely been violently snatched from his mouth. I had no choice but to believe his story, besides, this was too fantastic a story for a ten year old to make up. Refocusing my attention back to him, I asked, *Will you take me to your home, if I make it to the laundry chute?*

With bony, limp arms around my neck, he'd buried his little head deep into my chest and fell fast asleep. I laid there feeling like the little guy's protector, wondering just what to do. Completely exhausted, and cradling the boy as if he were my own, I drifted off to a quiet, restful place in my mind and gave into a deep sleep....

Chapter 6

"Outside for a Day"

The next day, I awoke to the bright light of the sun as it peeked its way through the open blinds.

"Good morning Mr. Broadhurste, how was your evening, did you sleep well?"

It was Nurse Helen; Red. The little boy was nowhere in sight and the closet door was closed.

Good morning Nurse Helen, my evening was very strange and no, I didn't sleep well.

"What do you mean, strange and why didn't you sleep well?" she asked.

I paused for a moment, thinking of whether or not I should trust her with my new found information.

It's nothing, I said, *I've just been thinking about my wife and what's come of her.*

"Oh I'm sorry, I wish there was more that I could do," she said. With that she changed my dressings and helped me to the bathroom where I had begun to wash myself. Changing the sheets she asked, "What did you mean by strange?"

Sensing that she was not going to let go of this line of questioning, I probed her loyalty to the hospital with a few questions of my own.

Could I ask you a question, Nurse Helen?

"Sure," she responded.

How do you feel about the hospital leaving patients on their own to die with no medication or treatment of any kind?

She stopped and came over to the bathroom door.

"I think it was simply dreadful what they did to you and what they're doing to other patients."

Then why don't you say something?

"Because this is a very prestigious hospital and I am only a second year nurse here, no one would listen to me over the word of the doctors or any administrators."

So you do think something is wrong here? I asked.

"Yes, but I wouldn't say anything outside of this room."

With that we began my therapy. Still unsure of telling her about the kid, I asked more questions as I came closer to trusting her.

I never did thank you for saving my life nurse Helen, if it weren't for you I'd be in the freezer down stairs. It is a little late but thank you for giving me my life back.

With a huge smile she said, "My pleasure, Mr. Broadhurste, my pleasure."

Nurse Helen did you ever stop to wonder why there are so many bodies in the freezer, I thought they would go to a funeral home or something?

"Yes, I have wondered, but it's not my place to question things like that, and neither should you."

Well, why not, is something bad going to happen to me if I do?

"You're talking foolishly now, it's best if we didn't discuss this any more."

Are you angry with me? I asked.

"No," she said, "I just wouldn't want anyone to overhear us talking and maybe say something to the wrong person, like my boss Dr. Michaels."

OK, I said. *I'll wait until we're sure that we're alone.*

With that she smiled and said, "By the way, I have a surprise for you."

A surprise, for me, really, I said, trying not to show too much excitement.

"Really," she said, "it's for you." She proceeded with, "The doctor has said your susceptibility to infection have gone down, which means your less likely to contract disease."

Oh, thanks, I replied, trying not to show too much disappointment. *That's a wonderful surprise,* I added.

"No, no, silly, that's great that you're progressing in all but what it really means, and your surprise, is that you can now go outside and get some fresh air."

Really, I shouted.

"Absolutely," she said.

Like a child on Christmas-eve I said, *Can I go out today?*

Any time you're ready," she replied.

Then I'm ready right now, ok?

"Yes, that's quite ok. I'll just need to get your chair and we can be on our way."

For the first time I realized that I had no clothes for the outside as I have been wearing hospital garments for as long as I could remember. Without giving it a second thought I sat down in my awaiting chariot and prepared for my tour of the grounds. Jokingly Red kidded, "Hold on to your stuffing, I've been known to break a speed limit or two."

Excellent, I replied.

And away we went.

Dr. Michaels' office is just up those stairs and off to the right isn't it? I asked.

"Yes it is, but don't be getting any big ideas, at least not right now."

At least that sounded as if there was still hope that she would help me get into his office to access his files.

What time does he usually leave for the day? I asked.

"I believe he leaves around six or so. I suppose it depends on his daily schedule," she responded.

Having made our way through the long hallway on my floor and past the nurses' desk, Red reached out to push the down button beckoning for the elevator.

"How did you know where Dr. Michaels' office was any way?" she asked, in a suspicious voice.

Without answering her question I responded, *Listen Nurse Helen there's something going on here and it's not good.*

"What do you mean 'not good', what's that mean exactly?" she retorted.

The elevator doors opened and she wheeled me into the farther most corner then turned me around to face the door. With a few people on the elevator she leaned over my shoulder and whispered in my ear, "This is by no means finished mister." With a curious smirk on her face she returned to her erect position behind my chair.

The doors opened revealing a large lobby with marble pillars and shiny floors as the assiduous onslaught of hard heeled shoes filled my ears. Busily tending to their respective crises and issues, the herd of people seemed to stomp by each other as if each of them were the only ones there. Seemingly avoiding eye contact at all costs, faces seemed to turn even if it looked like someone was about to acknowledge the other. This was a strange scene indeed, but I thought, no stranger than all that's happened in this hospital so far. Headed steadily for the front doors of the main entrance, Red pushed in silence. Finally we escaped the dull hue of the hospital lobby, transcending into another universe. This universe was filled with abundant sunshine and the sweet smells of pollen and blooming flowers. The birds were chirping and flying from branch to branch as they engaged in their routine mating rituals. Captured by the tranquility of the moment, my immediate problems began to subside and I welcomed the beauty of nature. This natural elixir of sunshine and harmony was just the thing for an ailing soul.

Rolling slowly but steadily, we passed a bed of flowers and potted plants. I asked Red if we could stop for a moment. Within this bed of flowers I found hope as I immersed my mind deep into its forest of green leaves. With yellows, reds, purples and blues this bed of life erupted into a kaleidoscope of bountiful color. Without speaking a word, I gave Red a nod; with that she resumed the tour. Passing the parking lot and around to the rear of the campus, we headed for the pond. Joggers circled the pond at a steady pace as the ducks scattered, giving them access to the concrete running path. With the normalcy of a typical day, my new surroundings reminded me of a time when life was sweeter and much more gentle. It became even harder to comprehend what I knew was actually happening behind the walls of this so called prominent and well respected institution; when the real terror lay in the things that I didn't know. It didn't take long at all for my new found calmness to wane. Thinking about my visitor last night, I felt the darkening clouds of despair begin to congregate between my temples. In an instant this once serene vision began to give way to the reality of my continuing plight. *Just what should I do about what the boy told me, if any thing?* I thought. *Indeed what could I do?* I wondered if I should confide in Red. Perhaps this was exactly what I needed to convince her to help me search for Christine.

Nurse Helen wheeled me to a bench on the running path just outside of the grasses' edge. There she took a seat. Facing the pond, she said, "You know, you really are a remarkable person and I admire you a great deal."

Thank you Nurse Helen, I do appreciate that, but I'm not sure that I deserve such praise.

"Sure you do," she said, "I can only hope that if God forbid, I'm facing a terrible crises that I handle it as well as you have."

It hasn't been easy. So many times I've tried to give up, I tried to give in, but I just couldn't roll over and go quietly into the night without a fight, even when I thought I had no fight left.

"You have a strength that others only wish they had, at least I wish I had it," she said.

My strength comes from the realization that if I don't do a thing then it may never get done, therefore, if I really want it to be done I had better at least attempt it myself. Those weeks in isolation, I had to come to grips with my mortality, with my God and my demons. The meeting and merging of all three resulted in my metamorphosis as it stands today.

"You see, Mr. Broadhurste that's just what I mean, how do you maintain such clarity while under such stress?" she asked with sincerity.

I hate to sound preachy or self righteous but our people have been doing that since we were brought here in chains. We search deep within ourselves for the resolve to survive and the will to rebuild. In the face of adversity we are taught to employ humility with dignity and to guard against the loss of our humanity. If you recognize strength in me it's the strength of an entire people that you really see. That borrowed strength is probably why I'm alive today. Of course, your help was invaluable. That's the end of my sermon, I said. Then added, *I didn't mean to rattle on that way.*

"It's wonderful," she said, "That you know yourself so well and that you feel a sense of connectedness to your people."

With a heaving chest full of pride, I responded, *I do feel that connectedness, and it will be the lack of it in us all, that will be our eventual undoing.*

Looking toward the pond we both stared out to the horizon without making a sound. Thinking about my wife, I reflected on how we used to take long walks together on the beach or wherever we could. I missed her terribly as I struggled to accept that in all probability she's no longer amongst the living. That made me sad for sure but it did comfort me a bit to think of her as having gone to a better place rather than having to relive our grizzly nightmare over and over again, as I do. As I closed my eyes, I felt the warm touch of Red's hand gently wipe away the tear that fought so hard to escape from my grasp.

'Red.' I'm sorry, I mean Nurse Helen, I said apologetically.

With a warm lighthearted laugh she said, "How long have you been calling me Red?"

Since the first time I saw you, back before I knew your name, I hope you don't mind?

"How could I mind, my hair is fiery red and you didn't know my name, besides, that's what some of my old friends in Houston used to call me. It's quite alright, really. In fact, why don't you drop this nurse Helen stuff, just call me Red. You are my friend aren't you?"

Yes, I am your friend, I'll call you Red. Besides it wouldn't be much of a stretch since I've been calling you Red in my mind from the very beginning.

"Then it's settled," she said.

Yes, it's settled, I replied.

"Do you always have to have the last word," she joked.

It's just the over flow from when I couldn't speak at all.

"That's right," she said, "You've recovered so well it's hard to believe you are the same guy that I was suppose to push into the meat locker, I mean the morgue."

You had it right the first time, meat locker.

We talked about just what was going on in my mind during that entire period. She even described to me how terrified she was that afternoon when she saw my eyes move, as if I didn't already know. *Red,* I said, *can I tell you a little story?*

"I'm all yours," she said, in a soft and delicate voice; one that seemed to say more than what was on the surface. I paused for a moment as I began to feel a strange closeness to her. I described to her the night that I was startled by the strange noises outside my room door; how one of them looked in my room. I further described to her how I was pinned down in the hall on the third floor and how someone opened the locked door from the other side. From there I described in detail how I met Nathaniel, the kid. How I found out later that he was the one who unlocked the door when I was trapped in the hallway. By the end of that story she was quite pale.

"How can that be?" she said in disbelief. "How can so much be going on in such a prestigious hospital," she asked.

I don't know for sure how, but I do know that something very strange is going on here. Red, that's why I need your help, I want to find out just what it is that's going on, and how they're getting away with it. Every day I'm more convinced that they have something to do with my wife's disappearance.

I reached up to wipe the tears from her face when she cupped my hand with hers and rubbed her cheek tenderly against the back side of my hand.

Suddenly without warning a shouting Dr. Michaels called out to Nurse Tate. Shattering our tender moment he stopped directly in front of the bench, eclipsing our view of the pond.

"Mr. Broadhurste, how are you this fine morning?" he shouted.

I'm better Dr. Michaels, thanks in large part to you and your great staff, I responded, as I looked in Red's direction.

"I see Nurse Tate has brought you out for a stroll. Enjoying yourself thus far?"

Looking at Red now I said, *yes, things are improving very nicely.*

"I'm glad to hear that," he said, "however I do have a serious matter to discuss with you."

Go on Dr., I said.

"It seems that both of your kidneys have been badly damaged due to your initial internal injuries. Tests show that one of them, the left, needs to be removed immediately before it collapses completely and begins to poison your system. The other seems to be responding to drug therapy. I'm quite sorry to be the bearer of bad news."

Then he unfolded his arms and reached for the chart he'd since placed on the bench. It was then that I noticed his badly bruised pinkie finger. The nail was completely black, presumably full with blood. Noticing that I'd noticed his finger he told us both that he had gotten it caught in his car door a few days ago. With that he shuffled his notes, organizing them in his hands and walked away while gesturing good bye.

As I turned from his direction my eyes fell first on Red, then out again to the horizon, I was terrified. Reflecting on what the kid told me about the others having their body parts taken and sold, I vowed that I would not become just another unwilling organ donor. I shut my eyes tight as I began to close in on myself, a feeling that was now as familiar as my name. Spiraling downward fast, I rested my head on Red's chest as she welcomed me with a warm embrace.

"Things will work out for you, I promise," she whispered.

Rubbing my temples and gazing out at the pond she said, "Now let me tell you a little story Mr. Broadhurste. There was once a patient in this hospital, a woman. She stumbled in one day covered in her own blood and babbling on about needing to get it out, or something. "Get it out of me," she would scream over and over again. A small child, a boy, dragged behind her like a lost puppy. The woman was badly hemorrhaging when finally she collapsed to the floor. The boy just stood there trembling but said nothing. A couple of orderlies reached her first. Lifting her together, they placed her onto a gurney. The woman fell flat, flinging open her blood soaked trench coat revealing a large and swollen stomach, about eight months worth, indeed, she was pregnant. They couldn't tell exactly where the blood was coming from particularly because a great deal of it was high above her uterus, splattered as high even as her chest and throat. They finally got her into the OR and prepped her for immediate surgery. The surgeon cut away her clothes revealing the full extent of her hemorrhaging. Stunned, the surgeon removed the largest strips of fabric as he opened the women's legs, placing them one at a time into the stirrups. It seemed she had multiple lacerations, deep stab wounds, in and around her vagina. In the course of normal operating room chatter some of the surgical team members began to speculate. As the doctor prepared first to stop the bleeding then to prepare for an emergency cesarean, he leaned in toward the huddle of his team and said, 'don't bother speculating, I found the knife in her coat pocket.'"

"They later discovered that she'd been here at this same hospital some eight months or so prior. Only then she came in after having been savagely beaten and gang-raped. Some skin heads, I'm told, stalked her one day as she was coming home from work. After they did their dirt they left her for dead. Not long after being treated and released from the hospital she soon recovered, physically at least. Emotionally however, she began to die inside, simultaneously a life began to grow within her. Feeling trapped and uncertain she tried desperately to cope with her lingering dilemma. Having had a strict and moral upbringing, abortion was against her religious beliefs, and all but out of the question. However she knew that she could never love a child spawned of such filth. She hated what they took from her and would therefore hate what she got from them. Consequently, she vowed to abort. Actually making it into the clinic at least five times during her pregnancy, only to turn and head home in exasperated shame. Continuing to torment herself she failed to reach a decision and missed her final deadline for having the procedure; thus she was forced to carry the child to term. Having had a very hard pregnancy both physically and emotionally, her pain and anguish would reach a feverish pitch. Over ten times she would stab deep into her own womb, missing the fetus only by centimeters. Tormented into an emotional frenzy she somehow made it into the hospital that fateful day," pausing to regain her composure, she continued.

"On August 2, 1972 she gave birth to a baby girl, five pounds, nine ounces. The child was a preemie but fairly healthy considering the circumstances. So too did the woman survive, though she'd never be able to bare children again. She stayed in the hospital for a few weeks, eventually making a full recovery. Not long after she vanished without a trace. No one saw her again including her daughter."

As she paused again, I thought to myself, *she couldn't be the woman, or could she?* She was obviously shaken by her own story so it had clearly registered personal for her. Sensing how fragile she'd become, I gently asked, *Do you know anything else about her, how old she was or perhaps a name, any of those things?*

Red responded, "She was about twenty seven at the time, some twenty five years ago. Her name was Rebecca Tinsley. She lived a simple and uncomplicated life. Going to work six days a week, twelve hours a day to make ends meet for her family. She even found time to take night classes at Bethune Cookman College. Rebecca Tinsley was a beautiful, single parent of two. She was African American with very fair skin and hazel eyes. She had a very strong work ethic and wanted more for her family. Rebecca Tinsley was very well liked and respected in her community. Rebecca Tinsley was also my birth mother. I am that unwanted child spawned of filth." She continued, "I had been raised to be a good little, 'White Christian' girl as my adoptive parents are lily white and very religious. I've always had very fair skin, freckles and this god awful red hair, passing for white was easy, up until I turned eighteen. At that point, I began to feel as if I had been denying a huge part of me from ever coming to the surface. I didn't always know that I was black, but when I found out it was like I wasn't even surprised. I can't explain it but that's how it was. It was on my eighteenth birthday that I found out I was adopted. It wasn't until one year later that I would find out the details of the adoption. At that point I found out about my mother and that she was black. I thought about it often over the next few years. Unable to leave things be, I finally broke down and hired a private detective to find my mother's family. Within months, I found them in Florida. Living in Houston at the time, I flew to Daytona Beach, where they live and I haven't left since. That was two and a half years ago. I learned that this was the hospital that I was born in so I applied for a nurses' position and was hired."

"Since I've worked here I've begun to notice some very peculiar things, things that I just couldn't explain, and now I still can't. Just as when you asked me to check around about Christine, I told you that I discovered some kind of cataloging files. What I didn't tell you is that the files contained hundreds of names with tissue type, blood type, sex and a list of, 'Undamaged Organs'; these organs had corresponding price tags." It's not that I don't believe you about the little boy, in fact I do, but now I'm more terrified than ever. I'm afraid that this hospital is much more than a hospital, I think it's also a bank, an organ bank, perhaps an illegal one at that. I know something very evil is going on here and I will help you get at those files, for sure I will. Let's just hope for the best in regard to your wife. I'd also like to see if there is any information about my birth mother, I sure hope not."

She leaned over, kissed me on the cheek and patted my hand, as her face bore the markings of deep fear and uncertainty. For the next thirty minutes or so we stared out into the still pond. With ducks floating and runners passing by, we sat in reflective silence. It seemed there was enough misery to go around. Red's pain was so obvious now, yet there was very little that I could do. My cache of pain and sadness would constantly remind me of my own troubles. I felt her pain for sure and it was heaped on top of a growing mountain of turmoil.

The sun was shinning softly through a thin layer of clouds, and the sweet aroma of the many flowers seemed to lessen. A stiff breeze would occasionally test the resolve of a few withering leaves as they broke from their once secure place in the trees. Littering the well manicured lawn, they fell helplessly to the ground. Never again would they absorb the life sustaining juices of the host tree. *Was I to find myself among the leaves,* I thought. *Had I too fallen from the life sustaining vines of my own tree? Had I as well succumbed to the ever stiffing winds, marking my death even before I reached the ground?* Once again, I felt the weight of the heavy doors of despair begin to close in on me. Not able to muster up a strong defense, the doors sealed shut. Waiting for me was the silence and darkness of solitude. With the strangest sense of familiarity it beckoned to me like one would to an old friend. Indeed, they knew me all too well.

My demons had returned!

Chapter 7

"Access To The Files"

On the way back to my room hardly a word was spoken. Caught in the vice of depression, I watched as the beauty of the moment splintered into reflections of pain and sorrow. Unable to rid my mind of the clutter of despair, I continued to sink even deeper. Thoughts of the operation that Dr. Michaels said was necessary further fueled my anxieties. I was coming apart, and I had no idea how to handle it.

As Red continued to push my chair across the grounds, I began to notice a heavy presence of security. Perhaps I was too excited to notice before, but it was quite obvious to me now. It seemed like they all were looking at me as if they knew something that I didn't. It was all so surreal, like I was in some sort of dream state. The faces seemed to come in and out of focus, while the voices were distorted, much like a record being played on the wrong speed. We made it back to the lobby of the hospital just as the clouds opened up, showering the grounds with what I felt were tears from heaven. Having been caught by more than a few drops from the crying sky, I began to awake from my foggy haze. All was not well, but at least all was clear again.

Just inside the lobby, I asked Red if we could stay awhile. She said it was fine, that we couldn't stay long because she had her rounds to make. Seated in clear view of the large, glass automatic doors, I watched as the down pour pelted the ground. And in the tiny river of water that ran down the concrete path, I saw myself being slowly washed away from what I once knew myself to be. After a few moments of quiet, reflective thought, I told Red that I was ready to go. Without a pause, she grabbed hold of the handles on the back of my chair, and we were in motion.

As the wheels of the chair rolled closer to the elevators the crowded lobby was a buzz. The same distant look as before appeared on the faces that scurried about. Pushing me into the empty elevator, Red patted me on the shoulder while pushing the button for the second floor. Not having said much since we were on the trail, she began to speak in a very soft voice.

"I know I haven't been very good company William, but there's so much to digest, It's a bit overwhelming you know. I hope you understand?"

Of course I do, much more than you know, I responded. *I know this may be poor timing, but I still desperately want to take a look at Dr. Michaels' files; in fact, now more than ever. Dr. Michaels will be scheduling an operation for me soon and I need to know before then. I really need your help. I probably won't be able to do it without you. Helen, will you help me, please?*

There was no response.

She continued to push me down the hallway towards my room without speaking a word. Barely making eye contact, she helped me out of my chair and into the bed. Pouring a glass of water she said, "Here's your medication, try to get some rest." She then grabbed her things, and without saying a word, walked to the door. Stopping midway she turned and said, "I'll see if I can pull a double shift tonight but I'm not making any promises." Before I could say thank you, she was off.

Grateful that she would even consider helping me to hatch such a plan, I felt the least I could do was to put some thought into it. So for the rest of that afternoon and into the evening, I constructed a well structured but flexible plan to access Dr. Michaels' files. After going over the plan at least a dozen times in my mind, I turned my thoughts to my clandestine accomplice. I wasn't sure as to why this woman would risk so much for me, but I found myself much more grateful than curious of her motives. Besides, I've often been told not to look a gift horse in the mouth; to accept your new found fortune, and get on with it. With that in mind, I calmed myself down and tried to relax. The sun was no longer anywhere to be found, and no stars or moon would shine that night. There was just another gloomy sky with dark shadows of clouds and a splash of light from distant lampposts.

As the clock on the counter read nine pm., my already jittery stomach became more uneasy as the possibility of Red not showing loomed large. Wasting no time, I began to structure a new plan. I didn't think things needed to be altered too much considering I all but subconsciously planned for Red's absence. The only thing that would be different would be the way into the office. I was expecting to just unlock it with the key, as Red had complete access to his office, being his assistant. No matter, I would just have to find another way in, that's all, not to worry, right. *Just who am I kidding?* I thought. *How do I get in and out of that office without anyone knowing it? I'm sunk if she doesn't show and that's all there is to it.*

Just as my thoughts were beginning to refocus on this most crucial aspect of the plan, I heard a light knock at the door. It was Red.

"How's my favorite patient?" she asked.

Oh I'm just fine, I said, *How about you and your day, you seem to be in better spirits.*

"Quite." She then added, "My day was rather uneventful, I made my rounds and switched shifts with a girl friend."

Perfect, I said, *and Dr. Michaels?*

"He's gone to a charity benefit; he left about two hours ago."

Fantastic, I replied.

We took about twenty minutes to discuss the plan then off we went. Red thought it best to take the wheel chair, that way if we had to explain our presence to anyone we could play up the supposed severity of my condition. First we made our way down the full length of the hall way of my floor, past an empty nurses' station and to the elevators. Up to the third floor we went. There the elevator door opened and standing on the other side of the opened door was a man in surgical clothes with his back to us.

"Excuse me?" Red called.

As if startled, the man spun around almost losing his chart. With the glasses that were once on his face now resting on the chart, he juggled successfully to keep them from falling to the floor.

"Are you going up or down?" she asked.

Red shot a look to me signaling to push another button according to his answer, at least that's what I was planning to do.

Leaning forward he said, "I'm going down to the main floor." Noticing his overcoat draped across his arm, I reached up and pressed six before he finished his answer. Just as I pulled my hand away from the panel, Red said "We're going up but you're welcome to join us if you like?"

"No, that's alright, I'll just take the stairs, good night."

"Good night doctor," she replied as the elevator door closed.

Off we went, bound for the sixth floor. In a nervous, crackling voice she said, "Good thinking Mr. Broadhurste, good thinking." On the way back down, I pressed the button for the fourth floor.

"Why did you do that William?" she asked.

We have to go to the third floor so I think it may be best if I left the chair on four, just in case things get sticky.

With a nervous smile she said, "Again, good thinking, you sure you haven't done anything like this before?"

Maybe once or twice, I joked.

After returning to the fourth floor, Red wheeled me off the elevator. From there, we rolled on toward the exit steps. Suddenly a door flew open, smashing against the wall with a thud. Red screamed and jumped back against the wall.

The little lady emerging from the room also screamed; dropping the plate she was carrying. Rushing to pick up the plate for the old woman, Red apologized profusely. Meanwhile, the old lady began apologizing for not staying in her room like she was told. She begged us not to tell the night nurse that she was leaving her room, speaking broken English with bits and pieces of a language that I hadn't heard before. It may have been Slavic or maybe even Russian. After calming her down, we then assured her that we wouldn't tell a soul. She told us that she was on her way to see a friend. She said she sometimes leaves food on the inside of the stairwell on the floor. That she never saw who or what came for it, but hours later the dish would be empty. Both Red and I thought that was strange, but the little old lady didn't seem to think it strange at all. As we helped to pick up the remaining morsels of food, she thanked us again and proceeded down the hall. Turning once toward us with a wave, she continued on route to the exit area, placing the food in the staircase as she had been doing for weeks. We resumed our journey in the opposite direction. Reaching the stairs, we parked the wheelchair and began to make our way down the steps.

"We have to hurry, I'll be needing to make rounds in about thirty minutes," Red cautioned. As nervous as I was, it was fine with me to get this thing done and over with as quickly as possible. Reaching the third floor, Red opened the exit door and peeked into the hallway. Waving to me to follow, we just about sprinted to the door marked 3C, accompanied by the name, "Dr. Michaels MD.," stenciled on the glass. A few jiggles with the key and we were in. The office was quite large. First walking through the outer office, I followed Red to a second locked door. Quickly, she opened the door. We then rushed inside. Immediately, she closed and locked the door behind us as she did with the front door. Pointing to the computer, she looked at her watch whispering, "You have ten minutes, tops, I don't want to risk being caught by some other administrator. I'm not the only one with a key you know." Wasting no time, I made it over to the computer, quickly turning it on. *Is there a password?* I asked.

"I don't think so, he too lazy for that," she said with a smirk.

Looks like you're right, the desktop popped right up.

Searching from icon to icon I didn't see anything that would clue me in as to where to start. The first icon marked 'Patients' opened up a file that had another fifty folders in it. *At this rate this could take all night,* I mistakenly said aloud.

"We don't have all night," quipped Red, "Get what ever you can and let's go."

Opening file after file, I was sure this would take much more than just the few minutes that I had left, but I continued on anyway Most of the files I found only revealed the case histories of countless patients. Finally, I thought to make the computer work for me. Accessing a search program, I tried to first put in the term 'Jane Doe'. The computer screen beamed with hundreds of folders labeled 'Jane Doe', each with a four digit number attached. The numbers started at, 0001 and ended somewhere beyond a thousand. I then tried the term, 'cataloging files'. The screen lit up like a Christmas tree. *Now we're getting some where,* I thought. Piercing our forced silence clanged the terrifying sound of keys jingling outside the front door. Panic stricken, I hit the light and turned off the computer.

I thought you said Dr. Michaels went to a fund raiser tonight? I whispered in terror.

"He did," Red responded, "At least that's what he told me. I secured his reservations myself."

Then why is he here? I scolded.

"How should I know," she returned, "We have to hide, hurry."

Finding a coat closet we ducked in and prayed we wouldn't be discovered. I was scared for sure, but Red it seemed was terrified. I was sure that I heard her praying to herself that we didn't get caught. Hearing the outer office door open and then slam shut she grabbed my arm and squeezed for dear life. In seconds the inner office door was opening and then shut, accompanied by the sound of hard heeled shoes hitting the floor of the office. It was at that moment that I realized I had forgotten to turn off the monitor. There was nothing on screen, but if he looked at the monitor itself he would realize the little light was on. *We're done for sure,* I thought, *although I didn't dare tell Red about the monitor.* For a few moments there was no sound at all. He had stopped walking and the paper ruffling sounds that formerly accompanied the sound of his pacing was now silent. Not even sure if it was actually Dr. Michaels, I wondered, *Is it a janitor who decided to kick back and read a few things on his desk? Was it a resident who had permission to use his office?* Not willing to expose ourselves, we waited in silence. Soon, my answer would come. Again the silence was broken by the harangue of the telephone. Ringing once, twice and then a third time, finally the phone was answered. Picking up the receiver, the familiar voice of a smug Dr. Michaels said, "Hello, this is Dr. Michaels, can I help you?" Pausing for a moment he then said, "Just a moment please." Pressing a button, he placed the caller on speaker phone.

"Comrade, what of my merchandise?" the voice on the line shouted.

"What's the rush," Dr. Michaels responded, "we're right on schedule."

"My buyers are getting impatient, and your shipment last month was incomplete."

"Ivan, my friend, you worry too much, you'll have your shipment, I just need to tie up a few loose ends here in the states. Surely you understand?"

"It is my job to worry. It is not my job to accept excuses and if we do not get that shipment soon, it will be you who will be worrying."

"Listen, tell your people I'll send a half dozen corneas by special shipment tomorrow morning, free of charge, how about that?"

"Comrade, now you are beginning to understand the Russian way. I think I can persuade my people to have faith in you. I will look out for your generous gift. As usual, it is a pleasure doing business with you."

Then he abruptly hung up.

"Yeah, nice doing business with you too, you fucking maggot."

He then placed a call, saying, "I need six corneas packaged and ready for shipment by tomorrow morning. I don't care if you don't have enough on hand. Harvest a few more bodies you idiot, just have them ready by tomorrow morning."

With that he hung up the phone saying under his breath, "You just can't get good help around here, even if you pay dearly for it." Soon after he shuffled a few more papers, turned out the light and went out the door, making sure to lock up. Not until we heard the outside door open and close did we breathe a sigh of relief. For more than ten minutes, neither of us made a move. Eventually we pulled ourselves together, mustering up enough courage to open the closet door. He had gone. I tried to speak, but couldn't. Red, with tears in her eyes, looked at me and then to the floor. Without uttering a sound, we left the office as we found it. From there we made our way back to my room without incident.

Now do you understand? I asked.

"Yes," she responded sheepishly, "Yes I understand."

With a look of distress on her face, she raised her hand to her mouth to muffle her cry. She then hugged me as if it were our last goodbye and departed. Surprised, but not as shocked as she, I laid in my bed with the lights off as I contemplated what I should do. *Indeed, could I do anything?* I thought. I had no idea how large this thing may have been. I didn't know who to trust. In some ways even, I wasn't altogether sure of how far I could trust Red. She certainly didn't do anything to deserve my distrust, but this whole affair was so bizarre that I didn't know what to think. Fortunately, I was temporarily rescued from my dilemma, falling fast asleep.

Later that night, the familiar commotion in the hallway came again. Past my door and down the hall, beyond the almost always 'empty,' nurses' station and through the exit stairs trooped a steady file of hooded figures. I wasn't sure why, but I felt compelled to follow. When the last hooded figure left my floor through the far exit doors, I was out of my room and hot on their trail. Up the stairs and through the third floor hallway they went, eventually disappearing into what I always thought was a janitors' closet. Needless to say it wasn't. That was how I learned of the overseers....

Chapter 8

"The Overseers"

The overseers had the art of subterfuge down to a science. As I quickly learned, it was a game; a game they arrogantly boasted to be a legacy inherited from the former slave traders of prior centuries. One of the many requirements of induction was that a new prospect need be a direct descendant of a well documented slave trader of long ago. If however, all other criterion is met without proof of having been a legacy, then a special tribunal would be held. It was such a tribunal that I had stumbled upon. This discovery was one that would haunt me for the rest of my life. The purpose of the tribunal was to give prospective members a chance to voice their strong sense of disgust and hatred for blacks and other minorities. Out of those chosen for most hateful content, one would emerge from the remaining dozen or so. He would be crowned king of the 'Exulted Order', a division within the group that spearheaded a drive to recapture their property, namely the Negro slave. It was the task of each finalist to illustrate how their actions in their community best followed the ideals of slave owners and traders of the past. In essence, they had to qualify as being modern slave traders.

One by one they proceeded in gory detail of how their actions helped to degrade and severely trample upon the spirit of the Negroes they would encounter. A military leader talked of how he systematically placed more colored boys than any other on hazardous duties. He further explained how he manipulated the testing parameters in a way that were designed for their failure. That anyone not able to pass this test by ninety percent or better would not get the option to pick his duty. General Oliver further boasted about how he was personally responsible for sending over five hundred black men to their deaths during the Vietnam conflict. Strategic placement of troops for all of sector 5, which consisted of over thirty percent of the combat zone, was his responsibility. He bragged, "I'd give the darkies a load of shit about protecting their nation, and those poor, dumb bastards would beam with pride as they marched to what would be certain death. The point man for every patrol was black or Puerto Rican," he said with a chuckle, "And as soon as they dropped down dead, I replaced them with another one. One day I lost so many of them niggers, I just plum ran out, had to sacrifice some of our boys for a few days till I got my new batch. That day the enemy beat us bad. The casualty count on their side was forty eight confirmed kills and ten wounded. Our casualty count was much higher; 'Charlie' had ambushed us while most of the camp was asleep. Our dead amounted to one hundred sixty two, ten of which were white boys, the rest were coons. I said a prayer for the ten dead white boys and secretly grinned to myself because I was there to witness the deaths of over one hundred and fifty niggers. It was one of the happiest days of my life," replied the general. He added that the little nigger children that these men had fathered would then grow up with no father, which surely, he felt, would lead to many other problems for those people. He continued to turn out more stories of horror, much to the delight of the panel of overseers. When he was finished, he thanked the panel for their time and consideration, raised up out of what looked like a dentist's chair, and walked out of the light, back into the shadows. An ebony figure appeared from the dark to escort him from the large, dark room, where he was placed into a waiting area. The heavy door swung shut.

Another dark figure appeared from the shadows and took a seat under the spotlight. He seemed to be a shy man with the mannerisms of a museum curator. He stated his name and slowly told of his occupation. He was a former school teacher who was also on the board of a historically black college. According to Dr. Hastings the best thing to do with those people was to study them. Put them in a classroom environment, straight from the ghetto and watch as they failed in droves and consequently lost interest. They would drop out, or often end up being expelled from the institution. Soon after, they'd return to their neighborhoods, broken with stories of how difficult college was, suggesting to their friends that it's better to pursue a trade.

He said, "While this group of dropouts was discouraging others in their community, my colleagues and I were busy identifying, 'tagging' those blacks that possessed above average intelligence. It was at that point, that the brain washing began."

He continued, "We systematically separated these students from the rest of the populous by inducting them into gifted programs. They are inundated with course work on history; American history especially. They are taught to believe themselves to be superior to other Negroes; that the only way to engage in any kind of intelligent dialog is to seek out white people for stimulating conversation. This not only further alienates them from their community but it also convinces some other blacks that becoming educated is a brain washing, or 'Selling Out' as they say. I'd like to share with you a case study on one Jimmy Taylor. 'Jimmy,' he said, was a very soft spoken, introverted black intellectual who was thirty five pounds over weight and going bald. He would wear the same suit most days even though he makes a good salary as an accountant. All of his neighbors hate him but that doesn't bother him because his fear of catching their ignorance keeps him far away from entering into any kind of dialog." He further added, "As if 'Ignorance,' can be caught like the common cold." This was another way for this sick genius to block the community's access to a well educated black mind. Inherent in the brain washing was the constant parading of historical notables that were known to have engaged in homosexual affairs. Jimmy was also gay.

Dr. Hastings replied, "Here we succeeded in placing the thought in the heads of these intelligent blacks that it was ok to engage in this aberrant behavior. This ploy serves several purposes. First Jimmy is further ostracized because he presents too much of an uncomfortable picture in the minds of other black men. Secondly, because he is gay it is less likely that he will father any children. And third, he is automatically placed in the high-risk category for contracting AIDS. To date, my staff and I have altered the life styles of several thousand black men, and we have very high hopes for the future."

Dr. Hastings calmly thanked the group and said he would be looking forward to their decision. He paused, picked up his tiny brief case and stuffed his pen back down into his pocket protector. Just as the last, he was led away. From there he was placed in a quiet room and instructed to wait there until he was contacted.

The next finalist was the President and CEO of a wildly successful chicken franchise, "Big, Jack Percy." Big Jack was a former chemistry professor at F.I.M. U. He was fired for experimenting on humans, mostly blacks. He said he wanted to know more about how they metabolized oils and fats. His original hope was to provide highly fatty foods that would serve to raise the blood pressure and clog main arteries. Much to his delight while studying the genetic markers for predisposition of hypertension and heart disease in blacks, he discovered what he described as a 'Magnificent Gem.' He found a way to rearrange certain natural chemicals produced by the human body. He then disguised these chemicals in the form of seasoning to add to his chicken. This particular arrangement of chemicals would effectively wipe out the Y chromosome in the sperm count of those males who consumed the treated food. He pointed out some amazing statistics of how the count of newborn black males had decreased by some fifty nine percent and the count of newborn black females had increased by thirty seven percent. Of course these numbers were for the state of Florida alone but he was quite optimistic about his country-wide plans of expansion. He determined that over the past fifteen years he had affected the outcome of over twenty five thousand births. "To limit the number of male children is to reduce the likelihood of strong leaders," he said. "We must keep the female as the head of the household. If we do that," he says, "We will continue to drive a wedge between black males and black females and of course without each other they don't stand a snowball's chance in hell of ever getting it together."

He said he was currently studying methods to chemically retard the growth of key brain cells in newborns, so as to substantiate the assertion that blacks are intellectually inferior to whites. With an arrogant little smirk on the face of this self proclaimed red-neck and bigot, Big Jack Percy stood up straight, tipped the right front corner of his cowboy hat and sashayed back out of the light, disappearing down a dark corridor.

I had estimated it to be well past midnight and it seemed a brief recess was called. The spotlight was dimmed and the whole room began to buzz with quiet whispers. It was a large room with a high cathedral ceiling. A hard wood floor and delicately carved cherry wood lined the walls. It was still fairly dark, musty and cold. There was an odd stench coming from the center of the room. It was a pungent smell of body odor, cigar smoke and urine. The walls seemed moist of humidity, yet through tiny glimmers of light you could see the breath of a few dark figures as they talked. The figures were in long dark robes. Hoods around the robes completely covered their faces. No hands or feet were visible as the robes totally camouflaged all parts of the body. Occasionally you could see the fingers protruding from the sleeve of a robe, tightly wrapped around a lit cigar. They seemed like monks busily moving about, stopping only to trade a few whispers. As I felt the moisture from the wall begin to penetrate my shirt, my body stiffened, as if turning to stone. My blood ran cold as I recanted the images just told by these most hateful, dreadful men.

How could any one hate us so much? I thought. *Weren't we the ones in chains? Wasn't it our woman who were used and abused, raped and stripped of their core? Wasn't it the essence of our people that was looted and pillaged? We are the people, who are the people, who are no more. We are the ones whose self picture was dropped from such heights and plummeted to such depths, shattering our canvass of existence into ten million pieces. We are the ones who routinely look at each other and see only that which makes us different. Could it be because we've lacked a true and complete self picture? Our millions of parts had to learn how to survive without their usual connection to the whole. Just as no two pieces of a jigsaw puzzle are the same, no two segments of a horribly fractured people would be exactly alike. We are the people who suffered the most from the execution of an old and well played military axiom, "If he can be divided then he can be conquered." 'Divide and conquer.' Surely as a people we are divided and we've long since been conquered. So why do they hate us so?* I wondered. *How many times can one lose? How many victories must they win?*

Completely befuddled and ultimately dumbfounded, I relived once again the tormenting visuals of my unending nightmare. My continued nightmare was sparked and set ablaze by the hateful words of these most despicable and loathsome men.

Eventually the movement stopped and all was still and quiet. No one was smoking any more so what little light there was, was now gone. There was a startling slam of a door and in walked another monk-like figure. Something was happening. The sound of his heels told me that he was walking in my direction. I was petrified. Sweat poured down my face and into my eyes. My body began to shake and it was all that I could do not to scream in horror as the footsteps were louder and much closer. I could feel my heart pounding stronger and louder, resonating in my ears between each step. Until that moment, I thought I had been well hidden. *They must know, surely I'm doomed,* I thought. Again, I was faced with an agony that was all too familiar; the looming threat of discovery and then execution of punishment. First you tremble in fear. You then shrink in spirit and personhood in preparation for the inevitable. A strange calmness begins to overtake you and finally you are ready. *It's right about now that you realize the true power of powerlessness,* I thought. *Since imminent death is upon you, you lay down your soul and open yourself for the taking.* With closed eyes and bated breath, I didn't dare move one centimeter, as the figure of death slowly strolled within inches of my face, passing by in a wistful gush of air. As the steady clamor of his shoes lead off in the direction of the group, my eyes swelled full, with tears, eventually showering my face with their load. With as much composure as I could muster, I carefully crouched down in the deepest corner of a shadow and cried the quiet cry of a shattered soul. I sat with my head in my hands and for the first time realized that I had been bleeding from my head and face. The blood was thick and sticky and it even had its own peculiar smell. That was the missing element behind that battery of odors in the air. I never knew blood had a smell, least of all my own. But this smell was curiously stale, much more pungent. It was especially strong in the area surrounding the pit.

Adjournment seemed near; perhaps I'd get to peer into this dark hole soon. I must admit that my curiosity was piqued and I really needed to know just what lay down there. As the figure made it over to the center, all heads looked bowed. With that they shuffled in closer to their center, surrounding the mouth of this great pit. Beginning to motion and gesture to each other they crouched collectively, taking on the shape of a huge dark mushroom. Deep inside the pit they stared and motioned with a draped, pointing hand. In an instant the huddle began to disperse while my eyes were firmly affixed on what appeared to be the leader. As he reached for a torch his robe fell back to the small of his wrist, revealing a Rolex clad white, man's hand, with a black finger nail, his pinkie. As if on cue this seemed as if it was revealed to me with purpose. Just as the figure switched hands with the torch he threw a decisive stare, dead on my position. I almost fell over from the impact as his silent stare hit me. It was then that the numbing revelation of familiarity began to sting, for I knew that hand; I knew that watch; I knew that finger they all belonged to Dr. Michaels. Standing waist high in a pool of fear, I choked down the need to gasp, remaining motionless, not uttering a sound. Without losing a stride Dr. Michaels' dark figure continued its steady gait off into the shadows. Ducking through tunnels and secret passage ways they scurried to reach the darkness. With no cloud of dust or commotion, the walls seemed to absorb them whole.

Into the dark, they vanished....

Chapter 9

"The Pit"

Still quite stunned and unable to move, I remained quiet for some time. The black robe clad figures had adjourned and now this moist-walled parlor was mine for the exploring. The room was still dark, still cold and still the stench of waste and other unidentifiable odors permeated the air. Listening intently for the slightest of sound, I began to hear rumbling from the center of this large and strange place. An orange colored hue began to make its way directly above the pit as it illuminated the ceiling immediately above it. Creeping slowly with the stealth of a cat, I made my way over to the mouth of the huge pit. The hypnotic motion of the burnt orange glow overhead told me the light must have been coming from a torch or perhaps several. As I came closer, the obnoxious odors pelted my nostrils and I felt my eyes begin to sting. Crouching at the edge of the pit, I prepared myself for the worst. Through glassy, stinging eyes, I stared deep into the pit. Almost overtaken by the smell, I leaned over even farther. There was just enough light to see the bottom. It was wet with a reddish brown liquid, perhaps sewage water that receded on the sides. The walls were made of rough cuts of blocked stone, much like the walls of a medieval dungeon. Alongside of one of the banks, I saw a large wooden torch stabbed into the side of the stone wall. There was no movement but I could hear a faint rustling off in the distance. It seemed this pit was a port hole or window into a tunnel of some sort. As the flickering light from the torch would rise and fall, it began to give way to more detail within. What I saw was now clearly a tunnel, *but to where?* I wondered. Now leaning into what seemed like the opened mouth of a giant, I stretched my body to gain access to the slimy and smelly throat that lay below. Tiring fast from hanging in this inverted position, the movement of a small but solitary shadow caught my eye. It wasn't particularly clumsy but it had no real grace to speak of either. As the shadow began to grow in size, I began to feel a knot in the pit of my stomach begin to grow as well. Slowly the shadow moved closer to my position. As I was at least fifteen feet from the floor of the tunnel I wasn't in any immediate danger but still I didn't want to be seen. The shadow began to take a clearer form. *It was some kind of animal,* I thought. On all fours it began to hasten its steps. I could hear the echo of splashes coming from just beyond my view. When the creature finally caught up to the darkness of its own shadow it stood up on two legs and revealed itself. Donning a familiar black robe, only wet with a pasty slime from the cavern floor, it stopped as it leaned against the stone wall. Counting my blessings for having the higher ground, I watched the creature in silence. Moving steadily towards the light it began inspecting the debris that lay in its path. Seemingly without discriminating taste it began to take its feed on something it found laying in the muck. Having a much better view now, I began to make out the shape of what looked like a human arm with the hand twisting and dangling by a thin piece of skin, With that the creature raised the arm to its mouth and bit a large chunk out of it. Having held back as long as I could, I felt the swell of acids in my stomach begin to boil over into my esophagus and up to my throat. As I watched the creature devour the human remains and all but choking on the stench from within the cavern, my mouth watered in preparation for the inevitable. Unable to keep it down any longer my body heaved upward as my throat erupted, spewing vomit in all directions. Uncontrollably, I sprayed the contents of my stomach into the mouth of the cavern. Coughing and gagging on my own bile, I pulled my torso up, out of the pit. Trying desperately to regain my composure, I looked down to find the shadowed creature looking up at me. Then in a high pitched voice it screamed and grunted as it scaled the wall in an effort to scrape off the remnants of my throw-up. Suddenly, off in the distance, I heard similar sounds coming closer from within the cavern. In no time the figure was greeted by at least a dozen of its cohorts, all scrambling to scrape the walls and floor for any morsel of my once ingested food. As the feeding frenzy lessened, the dark forms began to look up to me as if asking for more. A few even stretched their arms up to me, nodding and grunting as if trying to communicate with me. With several pairs of eyes on me now, my fear soon gave way to sorrow. How I wished I had some food to give to these hungry creatures. Still not sure what they were, I studied their form and watched as they began to drag themselves away. In a steady procession they filed out of sight. One after the other they took their place in line, like recruits on their way to inspection. Clumsily they marched to an unknown destination. When the last figure was ready to join in on the march, it looked up at me again, stared for a few seconds, nodded, and then reached for the torch. At that moment I knew for sure, the tale Nathaniel told was no tale at all, but merely truth. These were not creatures at all, they were human beings. As it reached out for the torch I could see a dark frail hand as it grasped the wooden handle. This little person, as I'm now sure, turned one last time in my direction, raised the torch and then joined in with the others as the light grew dimmer until it disappeared out of sight entirely.

Back in the dark I'd sit, wondering just what kind of hell did I stumble into? Barely able to see my hand in front of my face, I was stunned. Silence was all that I had left. My sensibilities have been taxed beyond comprehension and the limits of my imagination had been blown into a new dimension. I could feel my mind opening up to the hideousness of a strange and new reality. I knew then that nothing was beyond possibility....

Chapter 10

"My Confessions to Red"

After sitting in reflective silence for an hour or so, I decided to make my way back to my room. It took more than two hours to find the exact passageway that lead to the third floor storage closet. The many passageways lead to locked doors, some of which didn't even have knobs. Many corridors simply lead to dead ends. By the time I found the correct passage way, I was exhausted, barely making it up the steps; the same steps that sent me tumbling head over foot when I first followed the hooded forms. *I still don't know how I fell down all of those steps without breaking something,* I thought. I made it back to my room with little trouble. Of course my mind would not let me sleep, as it continued to switch from one horror to another; reminding me of my most recent barrage of twisted experiences. The words of those bastards, those monsters ranged in my ears like Westminster chimes. Their words would not stop pounding and pounding inside my head, as if its sole purpose was to pummel the flesh in my skull until it oozed from every orifice in my body. Not to be outdone by those God awful voices, the images of the hooded figures trying desperately to consume my throw-up, proved too great. I made it to the bathroom just in time, as I would not be able to stop myself from vomiting every time I thought about those images. *What do I do? Where do I turn? Who can I trust?*

I'm coming apart at the seams and I don't know what to do.

All I do know is that I've discovered such a hideous thing that I would have a hard time believing it if I hadn't experienced it myself. *How in the world am I going to convince anyone that this is going on?* I thought.

Like an old house, unoccupied for years, I sat vacant. A shell of the person I used to be. All that I was is now reduced to a hollowed host of memory banks, emotional turmoil and space. For the first time in my life, I didn't know myself. *What a pitiful state to be in,* I thought. My will to go on has lost its shine. It's no longer bright and strong. Now, it just slightly glows, with an occasional flicker. *I guess I'm finished. I tried to withstand these horrific trials, but I'm no match for them. They've withstood the test of time, and have rained down on the earth since the beginning of mankind, leaving scores of shattered souls in its wake. Surely, I am not expected to win, over such an omnipotent opponent.* Hatred it seemed was once again being declared the winner.

Vacillating badly in indecision, I sat motionless on the floor at the foot of my bed. Totally aloof but awake and yet curiously in a dream-like state, I gazed across the room. The fact that it was now a new day, registered only because my room was filled with thin streams of light that peeked through the partially opened blinds. Still dazed and unresponsive, I became cognizant only after being shaken by a very concerned figure dressed in white. Her face was obscured by the shinning light that filled my eyes as I tried to make out the features of her shadow covered face. It was Red. Still sullen and doom-filled, I remained unresponsive. I could read the words from her lips, only I could hardly hear her voice.

"What's wrong Mr. Broadhurste, William what's wrong?" she cried. Responding to this, I answered, *it's all wrong and nothing will be right again.*

"What do you mean I can't help you unless you tell me what you mean?"

There's so much to tell you, I don't even know where to begin, I don't know who to trust, oh..., I just don't know.

Throwing my hands up to my face, I just sat there shivering on the floor. Facing the wall, I tried desperately to free myself of the horrible flood of images, but I couldn't shake them.

It's all wrong and I just can't fix it, I just can't fix it.

"Fix what," she said.

Everything, anything, I just can't fix any of it.

"William Broadhurste, it's obvious that something happened since I saw you last, what was it, what happened? Please William; help me so that I may help you, please."

In a low and controlled voice I told her that she would not believe me, that I barely believe it myself.

"Of course, I'll believe you," she said.

But I was still convinced otherwise and did not dare trust her with what I knew. Besides, I still wasn't sure that she wasn't a part of what was going on. *Her horrible tale of her mother was quite convincing, but maybe I was gullible,* I thought. She did help me break into Dr. Michaels' office, but maybe that was part of their plan all along. I just didn't know any more. Up was now down; good was now evil and nothing made sense any more. Over and over I sat repeating, *It's just a bad dream, I'll wake up soon, it's just a bad dream, I'll wake up soon.* I learned later that Red had no choice but to call a doctor. The doctor gave me an injection of some kind, something to make me sleep I suppose. What ever he gave me worked.

Several hours later, I awoke in my bed with Red sitting on the edge. Greeted with her warm smile she leaned in to ask how I felt. Not responding she said, "Did you have a good sleep?"

I assume it was good, I can't remember anything, not even how I got into bed.

Red then told me what she had done and how alarmed she was.

"You were non responsive, not answering to anything, I wish I knew what made you that way."

No you don't, I said. *You don't want to know what I know.*

"Is it something deeply personal, or has it to do with the hospital?" she asked.

I returned, *it has to do with this hospital and it's deeply personal.*

Seemingly not able to interpret my answer she inquired further, "Just what does that mean, exactly?"

Slowly, I began to recant the horrible tale that ensued when I arrived at this hospital, as well as the painful events that brought me here to begin with. Methodically, I retraced the steps taken in vivid detail, including and up to meeting her for the first time. I gave a detailed description of the things that came to my door, the same ones that had me cornered. My thoughts then turned to the boy, Nathaniel. Unable to help myself, I would bare my soul. Sharing my hurt and anguish, I described his condition. How he exhibited animal like behavior because of the subhuman conditions that he had described to me. I told her that based on the boy's account of what was going on in the hospital; almost anything was possible, including the possibility that my wife was still alive somewhere in this madhouse. Then I leaped right into my most recently, shocking discovery. I told her of the dozens of tunnels in the basement and how there was a group of hooded figures that were connected to some kind of hate group. Red's face was as white as a sheet, but she told me to go on. I continued to describe to her the things that I heard them say about blacks, how they despised us. I told her of the bizarre contests held to determine which candidates best exemplified the spirit of the slave traders of long ago. At that point she burst into tears and ran to the bathroom. When she returned I asked, *do you want to hear the rest?*

"There's more?" she asked with horror.

Yes there is, I said, *much more.*

The monks in the center of the room continued to gesture towards the pit, I said, *which made me even more curious of what lay down there.*

After I told her that Dr. Michaels was among them, her face took on an expression that I had not seen on her before. She looked somewhat angry yet sad, and perhaps bewildered. As if in a daze she said, "go on." Having described how terrible it smelled and how damp and cold it was I started in about what I saw in the bottom of the pit. How the covered little person had eaten from a discarded human limb. I saw a look of disdain in her face, as she pouted her already frowned lips in disgust, but I continued on anyway. By the time I got up to throwing up into the pit, she was covering her mouth with her hand. When I told her of the creatures that scaled the wall in an effort to eat my vomit, she lost it. Racing to the bathroom, again, and just in the nick of time, she heaved from deep inside her stomach. On her knees she cradled the commode as she could not stop throwing up, into it. I wanted to help, but I was still a little out of it from the sedative.

Pulling the bathroom door shut she said, "I'll be fine, really, just give me a minute, thanks."

I gave her a minute, or more like ten. Eventually she emerged from the bathroom, refreshed and seemingly composed.

"Is that all if it?" she said in a strikingly calm voice.

For the most part, yes that's all of it.

"I don't know what to say, she said, it's all so bizarre."

Looking straight at her I said, *what can you say? That's why I was so out of it this morning, I'd simply reached my breaking point. One of many*, I thought to myself as I turned my hazy stare toward the window.

After staring out of the window for a few moments, I turned to look in her direction. Breaking the silence I pleaded, *I know it was a lot to ask of you to help me get into Dr. Michael's office and I know we were almost caught, but things are far worse than I imagined, you've got to help me escape this place. We already know they're stealing organs and selling them on the black market, but for some odd reason I get the sense that something even more sinister is going on, if you can believe that's possible.*

"But why do you think you are in immediate danger if you said that they didn't see you?" she asked.

I said they didn't seem to see me, maybe they did, and maybe I don't really need an operation, maybe that's how I'm to be

taken care of, on the operating table. I never did trust Dr.
Michaels something in his eyes seems cold and distant.

"Then why do you suppose they tried so hard to save you
once they knew you were alive?" she asked.

"First of all," I replied, *I was down in the 'dungeon' alone,*
receiving no medical treatment, left there as food for death.
Secondly, it was you who truly saved me and no one else.
Besides, I was so torn up inside, I couldn't have been worth
as much as I probably am now, all patched up and all, as
Nathaniel would have put it. I'm sure that I'm alive only
because someone has plans for me later, especially my
organs. Now I ask you once again Helen, will you help me?

"I don't know, I mean, I, I want to help but I'm so afraid, I
don't know what to do, I'm just so afraid," she said as she
tried to rise to her feet. Gripping her hand firmly I asked,
then will you at least promise me that you will keep my
secrets, that you will not tell any one about it, I mean no
one? Trying desperately to pull away from my grasp she
cried, "Yes, I'll keep your secrets, I won't tell a soul, I
promise, only please let me go I have to get out of here, I
have to think." With tears splashing on my linens she broke
from my grip and ran from my room crying hysterically.

What have I done? I thought. I hoped I hadn't trusted
the wrong person. I had little choice as I'd no other allies to
speak of, accept Nathaniel, the kid from the basement. I
knew then that I had to act fast, that I had to leave this place
with or without Red's help. Petrified and feeling so very
alone I cried aloud inside, but on the outside I would shed no
tears. I know now that I must replace my fears and tears with
actions, that without action, I would most likely become like
all of the rest and I hadn't experienced just how bad that
could be.....

Chapter 11

"The Fireless Flames"

The sun had finally gone down and the dark shadows throughout my room melted into a black shroud that covered every square inch within eye shot. In bed still, I laid unable or maybe unwilling to move a muscle. Drained, but unusually resolute, I continued to engage my heart and mind in search for the courage and wisdom to enable me to escape from this hospital of horrors. *It ordinarily wouldn't take so much strategizing and planning to leave a hospital, but with the security as tight as it is around the grounds, they'd never let me just walk out the front gate,* I thought. I was sure that if I were to be caught there would be hell to pay, and I'd been catching all the hell that I could stand. Drifting in and out of sleep, I began to think of Nathaniel, what may have come of him and what would become of him if I were to leave him behind. *I'll just have to take him with me is all, I can't leave him,* I thought.

My once level headed, cool demeanor had long since been replaced with nervous, unsteady trepidation. Unable to control the swirling undertones of panic emanating from my gut, I felt my throat stiffen and my chest tighten with pressure, as if I'd been wearing a thousand pound vest. Hardly able to breath, I gasped for tiny squirts of air, though not nearly enough as I could feel my lungs collapsing, draining them of all of their remaining oxygen. Unable to think of anything but imminent death, I continued to choke as my lungs seemed to be imploding. While heavy, warm tears poured from the corners of my withering eyes, I pounded my chest with my fist. Hyperventilating into a frenzy, I tried desperately to free my air passages. With my head now between my bent knees on the bed I tried to inhale as hard as I could, while coughing and gagging all at once. After fifteen minutes of stark terror and what I thought was surely the end, I began to slowly catch my breath. Wheezing terribly, I bobbed forward and back between my knees, taking in long deep breaths until my breathing returned to normal. And when I could breath again, I thanked my God profusely, getting down on my knees, giving her praise; then

I cursed her. *Why the hell didn't you step in sooner,* I scorned. For that matter, *why the hell is any of this madness happening to me?* Receiving no answers, I decided to stop asking God for hope and guidance, *I've been abandoned and it's up to me to see myself through this,* I thought. With this in mind, I decided to stop feeling sorry for myself, to get over my fears, and do whatever it takes to survive. Relaxed and calm, I leaned over the side of the bed to hit the light switch. As the soft light filled the room, I laid back against my propped up pillows in preparation for my grand escape.

Suddenly with a loud bang the door came blasting open, crashing into the wall. With my heart in my throat, I watched as two huge orderlies bolted in my direction. One of them grabbed me around my waist pinning my arms to my sides, the other delivered two hard blows to my face and head. Breaking free, I leaped to my feet, swinging wildly and missing my mark often but landing a few well-placed punches. As I advanced to the one in front of me, the other hit me hard in the temple, sending me crashing to the floor. There, I received a barrage of kicks to my ribs and groin area. Totally unable to defend myself, the two went on kicking and punching me in my face and head. They picked me up off the floor only to throw me into the wall, face first. Falling to my knees, I struck my head against the metal door jam. Finally, I landed squarely at the feet of a towering Dr. Michaels. Looking down at me he smirked, "You just couldn't leave well enough alone, could you? Now we've got to make an example of you." With that he delivered the final crushing blow to my head. Now semiconscious and bleeding all over, I was too weak to move. Pulling my body like a rag doll, the orderlies each took a leg, and at Dr. Michaels instruction dragged me through the hall by my ankles, leaving a trail of blood, they pulled and dragged me to the elevator where I lost consciousness.

When I awoke, I found myself in a tiny cell of some kind, completely naked and shivering from the bitter cold. I was in what could best be described as a concrete outhouse.

With barely enough room to kneel, I awoke with my knees pushed up against one wall, my shoulder wedged up against another, and my back but centimeters from yet another wall. The ridiculously freezing cold bit and tore at my flesh like vultures on the dead. The frigid air would lay frozen dew upon my skin, complete from head to toe. *The God awful cold cuts so deep and hurt so badly. Damn this wickedly sinister cold, damn you;* was all that I kept shouting. Helplessly I remained, burning from the fireless flames of the ice. All the while I was fully aware that there was absolutely nothing that I could do about it. Crying myself into a stupor, I screamed and hollered and begged, but no one would answer my cries. I knew then that pain and terror are both infinite elements in my universe. I've reached depths of each that have exceeded the darkest crevices of my imagination. Never before had I even considered the concept that I could be so cold that the effects would reverse themselves; that I would feel as if I had been consumed in flames that while hot, had no heat nor fire, but rather, ice.

I later learned that I would endure this mind bending torture for some ninety six hours more. It was then that I felt what little spirit I had left, crack and splinter into tiny fragments. *I am the man who is no more.* Over and over, I heard my mind speak to me. *I am the man who is no more.* Motionless and badly wedged in this concrete tomb, I gently began to release my hold on the pain. Releasing also, the fleeting hope that as long as I could feel the pain then I wouldn't have to go with the ultimate sand man, 'The Grim Reaper!' With twisted irony, the pain would actually bring hope, but now as I let go of the pain, I let go of all hope as well. *I am sure that I've finally reached insanity and it's somehow liberating, even comforting. Where would I be if I were sane? If I had to make sense of all of this, where would I be? I'd be right where I am, because trying to make sense of any of this madness will make you crazy and you'll end up right back where you started, getting acquainted with your new insane self.*

Sinking deeper into the clutches of madness I talked to myself for as long as I could remain conscious, cursing and shouting and crying like a baby. I whimpered myself into a new existence, one that was completely foreign to me. Eventually, there was no more pain and my body had completely disappeared, hiding itself especially from me. I could not feel one aspect of my body. My eye lids had long since been frozen shut, my muscles and bones were petrified in their places. *I'm here only because it's where I was last before I blacked out,* I thought. *I think I'm still here just like I think I'm still alive and not dead.* At that point I couldn't say for sure one way or the other.

Several days later, I would receive my answer. It came, as it usually does, in the form of excruciating pain. When I opened my eyes for the first time in almost a week, I was greeted by a calm smiling Dr. Michaels Again my face hugged the ground, but inches from his feet.

"Welcome back, he said, I'll bet you thought you were dead didn't you?"

Still in tremendous pain, I just laid there shivering on the floor of my new surroundings, saying nothing.

"Oh that's right you're probably in a great deal of pain. It'll pass in another few hours or so," he said, followed by a brief and sinister chuckle.

"Let me tell you what you have to look forward to. All of the pain that you've experienced while in the chamber, you'll be experiencing again, only in reverse. In other words, you're thawing out, and I understand that it's not a very pleasant experience at all. You see I've been working on new techniques in my study of Cryogenics. It's an amazing new technology. The idea of freezing live human subjects for later research has been around for decades of course, but until now, no one knew just how to revive the subject to see if the procedure was a success or not. With your help, I've proven my theories to be correct and I even have documentation. Sure there are a few kinks to be worked out, such as the extreme pain and degradation of muscle tissue, but we all have to do our part for the sake of science, wouldn't you agree? Besides you niggers should be happy to donate yourselves to scientific study, you're not good for much else anyway. Just think you all get to play a vital role in the evolution of man's mastery over life and death. Imagine being able to squeeze life from a living human subject, hold it in one's hand, and not surrender that captured soul to death, but taking it instead as your own possession. And when ready to restore life, I alone, without the power of God, will light the flame of life in this otherwise lifeless body of flesh and bones. That's the kind of awesome power that man has been destined to obtain, finally that hour is here."

All I could do was lay there, shivering on the floor as I listened to this raving lunatic. Marveling at himself, he went on, "I have effectively taken your life, almost literally held it in my hands, and then gave it back to you when I chose to. You were suspended somewhere between life and death as we once knew it. You should be grateful that I restored you with your puny life, that I had mercy on you. Most of the others were kept in stasis for many months before being thawed out. I've got special plans for you however, and you'd be well advised to follow my instructions to the letter. Remember, I own your soul, I own you. You are nothing. You come from nothing and I alone will tell you what you are, from this day forth." He then pulled back his right leg and sprang it forward, catching my face full with his black wing-tipped shoe. And in an instant, my lights went out.

Several hours later, I awoke to the menacing crackle of a fire breathing whip. The pain had begun to subside and I could see that I had been moved yet again. Through the tiny holes in the steel cage in which I was being held, I could see rows and rows of large cages, just like the one that I was in. On all sides as far as I could see there were these little huts that each contained something or someone. Although they sounded like animals, I knew different. I knew they were men, human, just like me. As the grinding sound of metal screeching against metal filled my ears, I watched the swinging doors to the many cages, as some opened and others closed. Under the constant thrash of the whip, I watched as a large dark man hoarded his herd of about a dozen or so people through the narrow alleyways between the cages. They were all chained to one another and wearing hoods and nothing else. As the sickening sound of this flurry of activity continued, I watched as many people, male and female, young and old, were herded from one cell to another. They came in all shapes and sizes, but one thing was common among them, they were all black. After each group grew in number they disappeared out of sight, off to unknown destinations. I couldn't believe what I was seeing. *This can't be happening,* I thought, *this just can't be happening. Not in America in the 21st century, this just can't be happening.*

Sitting in the middle of my cage, I began to question whether or not I was indeed still alive. None of us have died and gone to heaven or hell, then come back to talk about it, so who's to say how heaven or hell would manifest itself? I had no answers, not unless I chose to believe Dr. Michaels. *Nothing on earth can be as bad as what I've experienced, so I'm sure I must be in hell. Now that I'm here,* I thought, *I'd better learn to make the best of it. The problem is how, how do I make the best of such an absurd situation? How do I first get my mind around this hellish nightmare, that I should be able to better understand it?* Maybe that was part of the punishment that I never gain a true understanding of it, such that I continue to exist in an unidentifiable, never to be understood environment. Or maybe the soul and spirit have to undergo special doses of unimaginable peril, in order to drain the life out of them. Maybe that's just one of the many things that man cannot know and will not know unless and until he dies, taking with him the destructive secrets of "Sir Death." The secrets perhaps were those that would tell a tale of the demolition of spirit and the isolation and starvation of the soul. Maybe that's the way I am to be conquered, or maybe I've already been conquered and all of this is merely overkill; much like an extremely tasteless and tragic joke....

Chapter 12

"Cain and Abel"

Motionless, I continued to sit in the center of the cage on a floor of dirt and stones yet there was no sky above. The rancid odors pelted my nose and throat. It smelled as if I were in the middle of a herd of buffalo and it was almost as loud. As the putrid sounds of the outside commotion were deafening, they unleashed an onslaught of cries and screams of torturous strife. The whip was loud and all around me, as it hissed and spit and struck at will, like a Black King Cobra possessed. Biting deeply into the flesh of its victims, this possessed cobra would lash out at all in its path. Stinging my senses with every menacing crackle, I felt my body jump each and every time the whip made contact. Afterwards I'd shiver uncontrollably in preparation for the inevitable; in preparation for my horrible time with the whip, when it will eat of my flesh.

So I found myself again waiting for the worst to happen. With my heart bleeding of unimaginable fear and terrifying anticipation, I waited. Having no true recollection of time, I began to think back to my conversation with Red. *That's where I made my biggest mistake,* I thought, *I should never have told her a thing. I should have never trusted her.* As bad as things were then, they've gotten much worst now, at least ten fold. The only thing that truly surprises me at that point was that I was still alive. *Why am I still alive?* I thought. *What does Dr. Michaels have in store for me?* Just as I began to ponder this terrifying question, the door to my cage swung open. Crashing against the outside of the cage, the door clanged loudly as two large orderlies stepped in, the same two who beat me up in my room, both dressed in all white outfits.

"On your feet, monkey," the man on the left demanded.

Throwing a handful of rags at my feet, the other man quipped, "Put those on and get your black ass in gear."

As I fumbled with the clothes the man who threw down the rags smacked me hard across the back of my neck sending me crashing to the ground, hitting my head against a protruding rock.

"We ain't got all day nigger, now pick up the pace."

With that he gave me my first bitter taste of the whip, as it bit into my flesh. I was sure that I saw a flash of light as if there was electricity within the leather. Opening up an inch long gash on my chest, I watched the dirty rag of a shirt wick up the red tears of my wound, as the blood flowed freely from both gashes. On my feet and now clothed, but curiously unchained, I was on the move again. With one orderly in front and one behind, I marched following the direction of the leader with an occasional shove from behind. As I passed by cage after cage I confirmed my suspicions that they all would be chock full of people, mostly men but some were filled with women, most of whom were pregnant. They stood with a cold silence and a wide eyed stare, reminding me of the pictures I'd seen of Rwandan refugee camps, in a National Geographic magazine. I was especially touched by the face of one brown skinned girl who had to be in her early teens. Her face was blank and her eyes were swollen with tears but showed no emotion. As she stood against the front of the cage with her fingers sticking out of the small holes, our eyes met as I then realized that there was a man behind her having sex with her right where she stood. In the same cage there was a furious fight going on presumably to establish who was to be next in line for the girl. A deplorable sight for sure, but I could not stop thinking of what obscene plans were being made for me. As we passed through many corridors between the cages, I was almost knocked over by the smell. Looking down for probably the first time, I realized we were walking through human feces, urine and blood- soaked soil which was littered with smooth and sharp edged rocks. With bare feet, I continued to stroll through the muck.

With yells from the front and an occasional prod from the back, the forced march became even more brisk.

Keeping up with my new leader was all that I wanted to do at that moment, and thus I tried desperately to put all else from my mind. Failing miserably in that attempt my mind would insist on shouting to me, *Run you idiot, run. I thought sure run, but to where? Where in the hell would I go? And what will they do to me if I'm caught.* Surely, I didn't want to know, and thus, I ignored my minds commands. Trotting faster than before, I caught my toe in between two sharp rocks and fell to the ground, *I expected there would be hell to pay.*

"Get the fuck up maggot, we don't have time for this," shouted the man to my rear, as he leaned back throwing his right arm far behind his head. When his arm returned forward I watched as if in slow motion, as the curl of the dark leather whip took shape and then sprung out toward my face. Raising my hands and closing my eyes, the tip of the ferocious snake-like whip came slashing down across my left eye. Stunned and reeling with pain, I was sure that he had snatched my eye right out of its socket. Turning toward the ground, I grabbed my eye with one hand and tried to rise to my feet with the other. The blood just poured from my eye, through my fingers and down my chest. Grabbing onto a cage with my free hand, the whip came crashing down again catching me square in the back. Like a lightning bolt it fired its electricity directly into my nervous system, I was paralyzed.

"Now look what you did," quipped the orderly in front, "Dr. Michaels is going to have your ass for this."

"Awe, hell it's just another worthless piece of shit trash nigger, what's the big dam deal about this one any way?"

"I don't know, but Dr. Michaels said he had special plans for this one, and the last time I checked he was the one who signed my check, so back off, that is if you ain't already done killed him."

"Ok, you made your point. So how about we rest a minute and give this piece of shit a chance to catch his breath?"

"Fine with me," the lead orderly replied.

Laying flat on my stomach with my face partially dug into the earth, I laid without moving a muscle and without making a sound. Taking advantage of my rest, I silently listened as the two bragged to the other about their sexual conquests and how they dealt with niggers in their home towns. They traded short stories, joked and one even became angry as he recanted a story about how his ex-wife was a race trading, nigger loving bitch. That she married a nigger and now has two half breeds living under the same roof with his seven year old baby girl.

"So that's why you hate niggers so bad, because one of them is knocking off your old lady?"

"No," the man with the whip, replied. "Well, not completely but I got my reasons."

The other retorted, "Go on admit it you can't stand the fact that a *sambo* is fucking your woman, go on admit it."

He continued to taunt the man until he erupted, "Ok hell, I hate them all because one of em's fucking my woman."

He went on.

"She was having an affair for six months before I began to suspect anything. I'd catch her making phone calls late at night, you know stuff like that, until I stumbled onto a letter that she had written to him, dumb bitch didn't even hide it well. In the letter she talked about how she loved to make love to him, how his cock was so much bigger and better than mine—that she didn't know such pleasures existed. I almost blew my own damn brains out while reading the letter. I sat there with a bottle of Jack Daniel's in one hand and my nine millimeter in the other, thinking about suicide. Somehow, I came to my senses and I said 'fuck that,' I'll kill them both instead. Well, that was the plan at least. Before I could set it up, I passed out. The next morning I'd received orders from my company commander to report to the mess hall for emergency muster at o six hundred hours. Considering it was already five thirty a.m., I had no time to get myself together and get to muster. I lived on base so I didn't have far to go, but I was really trashed. I pulled myself together and made it out of the door and around the back of the house because I knew I had to puke. When I was done, I sat there for a minute sort of crouching down between the hedges and surer than shit this coon comes sneaking out of my bedroom window. Before I knew it, I was all over him. I mean, I beat the shit out of him. It turned out to be my CO. The son of a bitch was doing my wife in my house, in my bed while I was wasted downstairs. The bastard called this emergency muster just so he could get me out of the house, so he could get out before I caught him.

The Army doesn't take too kindly to striking an officer, so after my court martial, I drifted from job to job and started meeting with the 'brotherhood.' That's when I knew what I wanted, I wanted some pay back. I went to a rally here in Volusia County Florida, near Deland where I met Dr. Michaels. He had me checked out, told me a little about his operation, and then gave me an invitation to come work for him. The rest is history, as they say. So what about you, how'd you get into this business?"

The lead orderly responded, "I'm just in it for the money, I don't give a damn if its pigs, hogs, dogs, horses or any other animals. A nigger's just a coon and it don't make me no never mind what you do with him. So if I can make some money kicking their asses, hell selling their asses then so be it. Hey don't you think we ought to be gettin going?"

"You're right, we better get moving."

"On your feet soldier, you've had more time than you deserve."

Pulling me to my feet, the lead orderly inspected my eye, saw that the dirt had stopped the bleeding and repeatedly smacked me across the face, his attempt at bringing me back to my senses. Now knowing much more than I ever wanted to know about both of these social outcasts, the forced march continued. Having no idea of what was to come of me, I made sure to keep up the pace as the two began to break into a steady jog. As we snaked our way through the cages we finally ended up at the entrance of a cave. Stopping for nothing, we jogged on. We must have run for more than two miles through the winding hollowed out catacombs, when we came to a tunnel that had a familiar yellowish glow to it. Slowing down now, we walked through what looked like an observation area. Below us there were several dozen steel tables, all on a slight incline with a draining hole at their end, which was attached to a tube that connected to a plastic container. Each table was occupied by what some would call, a fresh kill, as the blood poured freely from each corpse. Along side each table were steel trays that stood on wheels. The trays were full of organs of all types. Some were in solutions of some kind, formaldehyde, I guessed. Others were simply lying on the trays in no particular container at all. As we passed by the people cutting and sawing the bodies they continued on working busily as if we weren't even there. Literally gutting the bodies completely and then taking inventory of its usable contents, the surgical team worked as if this was no different from any other warehousing operation. Meticulously they weighed, bagged and covered containers containing organs and tissue, labeled them and then put them into the glass-door refrigerated cases. With my own eyes, I was witnessing the ugly truth. I watched as they reaped their loathsome harvest and my blood ran cold as my brain could hardly process what my eyes had revealed.

After passing through this hallway of glass, we made our way to another dark passageway, where it was damp and cold. We quickly made our way through that passage way as it lead us to the foot of the steps, that lead to the janitor's closet. Through the closet, we made our way back to the drab hallways of the hospital. The overhead lights told me that whatever the time, it was at night, as I'd learned earlier that only one of the three panels of lights were on during the night hours. Quickly they hustled me up the stairs and to Dr. Michaels' office, where he was waiting, cross armed and evil grinned.

"Where the hell have you two been, don't you know we have a schedule to keep?" demanded a scolding Dr. Michaels, "And what happened to his face?"

"Well, he fell and hit his head and."

"Enough of your sorry excuses," interrupted Dr. Michaels, "Get him in here, you incompetent asses, hurry!"

With that, I was rushed into the office and the door slammed shut behind me, sealing me in and perhaps sealing my fate. After tying my feet and hands they put a noose around my neck and tied me to a post like a dog. By now so much of me had been stripped away that not much of whom I knew myself to be had survived. Like peeling an onion, my layers of personhood were cut to my core and then discarded like so much useless trash. *Doom and gloom is what I have to work with now and I see no end in sight,* I thought in silence. Whatever my fate was to be, I hoped it would come soon— I hoped it would be complete and final. There wasn't much left of me to take, nothing except my life and that didn't seem to be worth much any more, if indeed anything at all.

"You damned fools, I told you explicitly, 'No new facial wounds,'" I heard him angrily whisper to the men, "We may need him later."

They continued to converse until Dr. Michaels smacked the marine guy hard across the jaw. I could see the veins in the orderly's temples grow thick with angry blood, spreading quickly across his skin, as his entire head became flushed with a rich hue of red. Staring Dr. Michaels down, red faced and all, he clinched his jaws tight sawing his teeth slightly, but did not dare utter a sound. As the other man looked as if he wanted to melt into the fixtures, he submissively hung his head low, casting his stare off to his right, anything to avoid eye contact with Dr. Michaels. Seemingly scolded and disgusted, the two stood perfectly still, placid and silent. They did at least until Dr. Michaels exploded, "Get out of my sight." With the swagger of two brooding little boys they quickly strolled away closing the office door behind them.

Immediately, Dr. Michaels shot his cold stare in my direction. "So Mr. Broadhurste, how do you like your new accommodations? It seems you didn't like your nice comfortable room in H ward very much, at least you never wanted to stay in it. So I thought you could use a change of scenery."

Pausing to lift a chest from the floor to the counter, he then stopped, and looked at me with a completely blank expression.

Why me? I asked of Dr. Michaels, *why did you choose me?*

"Well why not you? Mr. Broadhurste?" Dr. Michaels replied, "Or should I say Mr. Dogan? Mr. Wayne Dogan. I know much more about you than you think," he said. "First of all, I know you're not William Broadhurste. You're not a thirty seven year old, six foot four inch tall, two hundred sixty nine pound white male with dirty blond hair, blue eyes, with a bullet lodged in the back of the head, now are you? I didn't think so. You show up one day in my emergency room bloody and badly beaten, wearing nothing except a pair of black, rhinestone studded leather pants. Inside the rear pocket was a black leather wallet. The wallet was the type with the chain connected to a ring in the upper left corner as the other end was connected to a belt loop; you know the type that a good old boy would wear. Inside the wallet was a West Virginia driver's license of one William P. Broadhurste. Curious, I'd find you wearing those pants with that identification, the identification of another man— indeed the pants of another man on your body, curious indeed. The plot certainly did thicken when several days later the police brought the body of a 'John Doe' to my morgue. He was naked from the waste down. William P. Broadhurste, alias 'Petee,' is dead. His body is frozen and still in my morgue and it looks like you killed him."

No, I didn't kill him, I responded in a weak voice. *It was one of his own, the leader. I would have killed him if I could have but I never got the chance, the man with the tears ordered him shot and I never saw the man's face that did it, the one who shot him from behind.*

"It doesn't matter much to me, but I'm sure the local police will be interested in your connection to their John Doe."

I knew what he was getting at but I didn't know why. *Surely he had the complete upper hand,* I thought, *and could crush me like a bug if he chose. Why then was he acting as if he needs something from me?* I wondered.

"So Mr. Dogan why would a murderer like you go sniffing around in matters that don't concern you? You would think you'd want to recover, mind your own business and quietly disappear. Why couldn't you have done that? Just what were you searching for down in the tombs?"

It was just as I'd thought, he knew all the while that I was sneaking around the hospital, he also knew that I was there in the large room where the monk like figures were huddled around the pit, I thought I was completely hidden. *It must have been Red,* I thought, *she must have told him everything that I ever told her.*

Dr. Michaels walked over to the sink, turned on the faucet and filled a glass to its top with water.

"Would you like a glass of water Mr. Dogan, you look as if you could use it?"

Yes I would, I responded, in the same low, hoarse voice that I had since they tied me to the post in Dr. Michaels' office.

With a crooked smirk on his face, Dr. Michaels walked back towards me, slightly spilling the water as he came closer.

"So you want some water do you? Here's your water."

He then threw the water in my face and smacked me several times about my head. Kicking me in the chest he said, "Why the hell did you meddle into my affairs? You, a fucking nobody; you would try and damage my life's work?" Striking me hard in the throat, he sent me crashing first into the wall then to the floor. Choking and gasping for air, I inhaled hard as I tried to re-inflate my lungs. With my wrists and ankles still tied, the noose still knotted firmly around my neck, my lungs would barely respond. I continued to choke from the original blow to my throat.

"What did you tell her," he yelled, "what did you tell her about the harvest? Do you have any idea who you're messing with, well do you?"

With his hands firmly gripped around my throat he shouted again, "What did you tell her? Tell me now or I'll break your sorry neck."

Tell who? I squeaked as he loosened his grip.

"You know who, nurse Helen Tate, what did you tell her?"

I didn't tell her anything, I swear, nothing at all, I swore to Dr. Michaels.

"Liar."

With that he gave me a hard blow to my ribs, knocking the remaining morsels of oxygen clean out of my body.

"The more you lie, you maggot, the longer this beating will continue, now what did you tell her about my operation? Tell me now," he shouted.

Trying to catch my breath, I responded, *I only told her about myself and my wife Christine, how we ended up in this place, that's all, I swear.*

"Liar," he hissed. He then reached in a drawer and pulled out that dreadfully ugly, black leather whip. Snapping it on the wall close to my head and then on the floor close to my thigh, the hideous tool lashed out a third time. Catching me behind the ear, I screamed in horrifying pain, begging him to stop. Relentlessly, he continued to strike at will. Every blow it seemed slammed harder and hotter than the last. The pain was constant and ever increasing. Trying desperately to cover my face with my bound hands, the whip ripped and tore the flesh on my forearms. The once white, tiled floor almost completely painted with the smudged strokes of my blood. My attempts of escaping the bite of the serpent were futile, as Dr. Michaels continued his onslaught of tyranny.

After what seemed like an eternity, he brought down the whip for the last time. Folding the whip into three or four loops he placed it back into the drawer and walked over to the mirror. There he threw some water in his face and then wiped off with a clean white towel that was resting on the side of the sink. Throwing the towel at my feet he said, "Wipe your face and stop whimpering, it's over for now." Still unable to stop sobbing, with clasped wrists, I wiped the blood and tears from my face while inspecting the deep bloody whelps that covered my arms and legs. Once again I was completely beside myself with fear and mind numbing pain. Not knowing what was to happen next, I sat quietly in the corner; still totally unable to process my descent into the ever present, welcoming arms of madness. Like a dirty junkyard dog, beaten for disobeying his owner, I sat there quite pensive, licking my wounds and trying not to flare the temper of the master. In every sense of the word, I was a slave. With a devilish gleam in his eyes, Dr. Michaels regained his composure taking on the look of a mad, maniacal scientist. Turning his attention to the chest on the counter, with his back to me, he began to survey its contents. Mumbling the word, beautiful, to himself he reached in and pulled out a cage. Putting the cage in plain sight, he revealed its imprisoned contents. The cage was home to one of the biggest rats that I'd ever seen in my life. At first I thought it was a small cat, but the long scaly tail assured me that my eyes did not deceive me. I don't know how, but somehow he must have known that I was terrified of rats. He picked up the cage and brought it closer to me. I thought to myself, *Please God, I'll take the whip, just please don't let him put this rat on me. I'll die, I know it; I'll just die.* Trying to remain calm, I stared at the large rodent, hoping against hope that Dr. Michaels wouldn't see the stark terror that invaded every fiber of my body and mind.

"How do you like my pet?" he taunted. "Oh you want to play with him? Don't worry, you'll get your chance, only he's a little cranky now. I haven't fed him in a couple of days, just a few scraps you see and he's quite hungry." Bringing the cage even closer he leaned over and said, "Would you like to pet him?"

As soon as the rat came closer it lunged at the cage hissing and biting the thin bars of the cage in an effort to strike at me. With a long metal rod Dr. Michaels began to badger the rodent, working it into a frenzy. The vile squeal of the rat filled my ears as it tried desperately to escape the confinement of the cage and the constant poking and prodding of the metal rod. Fighting off the rod, the rat snapped in all directions. Clearly agitated and showing his two yellow front teeth. Seemingly ready to sink them into any thing that it could get a hold of. Leaving the cage on the floor directly in front of me, Dr. Michaels turned and walked back to the outer office where I heard the whine of an opening closet door. Meanwhile, this oversized rat was moving from side to side, shifting its weight from one side of its body to the other as if readying itself for a fight. With saliva dripping from its mouth, it continued to hiss and snarl while staring me straight in the eyes. It would occasionally hook its teeth around the bars in front of its cage in an effort to get to food, and in this case the food was me. Returning with a second cage, Dr. Michaels scoffed, "You're in for a real treat." Spinning around as if presenting a gift, he then shoved the second cage in my direction. This sick bastard revealed another caged rat. This one was even meaner than the first and even uglier. It was huge, black, with a long, slimy, thick tail and a heavy patch of fur behind its head. Immediately they thrashed about the cage as they tried to get at one another. Squealing and jumping, they fought hard to free themselves from their cages. With my back firmly up against the wall, I watched as the drama of rodent posturing and intimidation played itself out. They were clearly the victors and their job was done, I was out of my mind with fear.

"Getting acquainted with my pets I see," he said with twisted sarcasm. "They're brothers you know, but they hate each other something terrible, so I've named them Cane and Abel."

Seemingly quite pleased with his attempt at being humorous, he quipped, "I guess you can tell they like you," with that he chuckled out loud as he walked back to the closet in the outer office. Fumbling around in the closet, I heard what sounded like the opening and closing of yet another cage. When Dr. Michaels emerged from the outer room he had an even more strange apparatus than I could have imagined. Bringing in a chair with him, he placed it near me and told me to sit in it. After doing so, he strapped me down with arm restraints and then duck taped my legs to the legs of the chair. Smiling and humming what sounded like Albinoni's Adagio, he carefully placed what looked like a circular bird cage over my head. Gripped with absolute terror, my body trembled uncontrollably as he locked the cage around my neck. It was a strange looking thing, something akin to a medieval torturing device. The bars were thin and strung close together, but I could clearly see out of it on all sides. There was no opening in the front of the cage but curiously enough there were two doors to the cage, one on each side, closest to my left and right ears. Before I could fully anticipate Dr. Michaels' next action, he reached for the cage of the first rat and began to do the unthinkable. With a few snaps and clasps the cage and its hungry occupant was fastened to the cage on my head. Now just inches from my head, the rat fought viciously to escape the cage. As it hissed and sprayed its spit into my eye this little monster was so close to my face that I could smell its breath. It was so close, I could even feel its whiskers every time it lunged forward in an effort to snatch my ear into its hungry mouth. Now totally unglued, I screamed in horrific panic. Not bothered in the slightest by my pitiful display, Dr. Michaels went about his business of hooking the other rat up to the right side of my cage. When the rats got wind of each other they immediately became uncontrollably violent, striking the cage with even more vigor. Shaking and twitching and pulling at the restraints, I tried mercilessly to free myself. It was no use. Squeezing its head through the bars, the rat on my left lunged tenaciously, grabbing with his teeth and then pulling a plug of cartilage from my ear. Hastily, the rat chewed its first taste of flesh. Banging my head as hard as I could against the cage on my left, I sent the rat flying to the back of its cage. Now that it had drawn blood, it seemed even hungrier and more resolute. I, on the other hand, was getting angry. Showing my teeth and hissing back at both rats, I tried to ready myself for the time that at least one of them would break free from their cage with the intent to eat its way through my brain. Each time either rat would come close to getting its head through the bars I'd slam my head against its mouth sending it reeling to the farthest end of its cage. Each time I was successful at preventing them from getting in, but they also were successful at getting in a quick, sharp bite to my skull before they lost their footing. Angry, but still petrified, I fought off my attackers every way that I could. I spit and shouted and shook my head as hard as I could as the rats went tumbling all over their cages. Totally consumed with the fight of my life, I continued on. Not noticing much else, not even Dr. Michaels when he reached out grabbing the center cage, I continued to shake my head and anything else that would deter the mad rodents.

"This is getting boring," he said, and began to open the cage door on the right. Pulling the door up slowly, the rat immediately dashed for the small opening trying to force its head under the bar as Dr. Michaels prevented the bar from coming up completely.

"Now Mr. Dogan," he said, "What did you tell Nurse Tate?"

Nothing, I said, I swear.

Watching the rat dash for the opening, I soiled myself, urinating and defecation right where I sat, right in my pants.

"Did you know that she's not really a nurse? Huh, did you?"

No, no sir, I didn't, I replied.

"She's really a cop and when we find her she's going to wish she'd never been born and that's a promise," he said. "And if I find that you told her anything about the harvest, I promise you a slow agonizing death; with modes of torture that have never been seen before in this country."

As if in a trance, my eyes dismissed the menacing rats as I prayed for my redemption. Unhooking the clamp around my neck, Dr. Michaels slowly lifted the center cage from my head. Replacing the bottom with another attachment, he then placed the three connected cages on the counter directly in front of me. Simultaneously he opened both side gates. The rats went charging at each other like two mad bulls. Locked in a bloody struggle to the death, they fought like Tasmanian Devils. Biting, clawing and completely entangled in the heat of battle, the bigger black rat finally delivered the fatal bite to the throat. As it bit and gnawed at the flesh of the dead rat, a few squirts of the losers' blood sprayed freely in my face. Feeling blessed to still be alive I hung my head and let out a sigh of exasperated relief. Having left the office entirely, Dr. Michaels neglected to untie me and left the cage in front of me, less than a foot from my face. There, I would continue to witness the cannibalizing rodent make a meal of his brother. As I tried to digest the absolute horror of what just happened, I shuddered to think that both of those rats could have been making a meal of my brain at that very moment. I don't know how but again, God continued to bless me with life. There must be a God somewhere because I was truly a walking dead man—one who had died at least a dozen times or more....

Chapter 13

"Blue Knitted Shawl"

Still tied to the chair and barely conscience, I could remotely hear a scratching sound coming from somewhere above my head. Too exhausted, I didn't have even enough strength to look up. Hearing the slight commotion grow louder, I felt the pulse in my neck begin to quicken against the thick leather collar. The familiar under swell of panic returned and again I fell prey to the firm grip of a gut-wrenching fear. It seems that no matter how horrible my most recent experience, the one to follow would only get worse. Taking in a deep breath, I tried to convince myself that nothing could be worse than what I'd experienced so far. But there I was, panic stricken again, and totally unable to control my shivering body. Just like the last time and all of the other times, I found myself terrified, yet still clinging to life. It was as if I were trapped in a maze and I, although frustrated and utterly destroyed, refused to give up my quest for freedom. As the muffled sounds overhead grew louder, I shut my eyes tight and braced myself for the worst. Then as suddenly as the noise began, it stopped. Silence began to fill the office except for the occasional ruffling sound coming from the cage. Cain was not exactly through with his brother Abel as he politely continued to feed on the bloody corpse, seemingly uninterested in anything else. Distracted by this spectacle, I was immediately thrown back to the terrifying moment of truth; the moment that Dr. Michaels threatened to open the cage door for the hungry victor, Cain.

Then without warning, I was yanked back into reality. With a loud thump, I heard something hit the floor behind me. Trying desperately to jump out of my seat, I fell to the floor still firmly strapped to the chair as it toppled over completely, breaking two of its four wooden legs. Almost succeeding at hanging myself, I quickly squirmed back toward the wall, lessening the tension on the chain that was still tightly fastened to the collar around my neck. Again, gasping and coughing to catch my breath, I stared across the floor of the office from my now skewed vantage point. Suddenly, out of the corner of my eye, I caught a flash of dark fabric, then the sound of tiny feet as they trotted through the doorway and into the outer office. I heard the door open and then close and didn't know what to expect next. In no time the sound of the feet returned and a small, fabric covered creature stood before me. Looking up and through a heavy daze, I watched as the dark figure reached up and snatched its hood from its head. There he revealed the wide and toothless grin of a familiar face. My terror quickly gave way to surprise and delight. It was Nathaniel. I had never been so happy to see anyone. Not wasting any time he reached for a scalpel that had been laying on the counter and cut me free from the chair. He then unlatched the collar from around my neck. As it swung away from my body slamming into the wall, to which it was fastened, I scrambled to get to my feet. As I reached out in an effort to hug my brave little rescuer, I collapsed to the floor. With Nathaniel's help, I managed to pull myself to a seated position with my back up against the wall. Tapping me on the shoulder he motioned above to the open vent, about six inches from the ceiling. While trying to speak to tell him how thankful I was, he quickly ran up to me and placed his small hand over my mouth. Then he raised his finger to his lips, whispering, "shhhh." Again, he motioned to the vent and pulled at my shoulder. I was so weak at this point; I thought I'd never make it up to my feet again, much less into that ventilation shaft. My left eye was swollen shut and the gashes on my arms, although no longer bleeding, were deep and still very sore. Reaching down, I struggled to force blood back into my ankles and feet. The circulation had been cut off for so long that I could barely walk I could hardly feel my feet at all. Realizing this may have been my only chance at escape, I tried desperately to stand. With Nathaniel's help, I was finally able to get to my feet. The task of reaching the vent seemed like an impossible one. Ordinarily, it wouldn't have been hard to reach at all, but I was in a bad way at that point. My body had taken a real beating. Hungry for freedom, I tried to muster all of the strength that I could, but to no avail. It was too high and I had broken the only chair in sight.

Luckily the boy was thinking clearly as I just couldn't. Just as I was about to give up, he came racing into the inner office wheeling a large back chair across the floor. It was Dr. Michael's desk chair and it was just enough to elevate me to the point that I was able to grab onto the opening of the vent and pull myself up. With just enough room to wiggle my body up and into the shaft I turned on my side and waited. Having pulled myself far enough away from the mouth of the shaft, I strained my eyes to see through the darkness that would await me. Waiting rather impatiently, I called in a brisk but muffled whisper, *Nathaniel, where are you?* I received no reply.

Nathaniel, I called, *we must hurry.*

Again, I would get no reply. Suddenly, I heard the squeal of Cain, the victor. It screamed once then twice and then no more. Seconds later, with a heavy thump I felt the weight of the now dead rodent as it landed smack in between my crossed calves When I finally realized what was going on, I panicked; thrashing my legs about, ridding them of this nasty little monster. Dead or not, I was still terribly afraid of this thing and didn't want anything to do with it. After he killed and tossed up what must be dinner for him or someone, he pushed the chair back to its proper place in the outer office, behind the desk. I could only see shadows from the shaft, but I could surmise what he was doing by the sounds of his flurry of activities. I then heard the door open and almost screamed out loud. Holding my breath and listening intently, I began to realize what he was doing. He opened the door and put back the chair to make it look as if I had escaped and walked right out the front door of the office. I could see now how this kid had survived for so long. He was smart, cunning and very careful. Lost in thought, I laid motionless, convinced that Nathaniel was taking entirely too long to return. Then suddenly without warning came a hurling Nathaniel. Up and through the opening at the mouth of the ventilation shaft he went. Carefully he pushed the sheet metal grill out of the shaft as he gripped the small bars with his tiny fingers. He then put it perfectly in place and gently pulled on it to secure it in place. Grabbing the rat by the tail and holding it up as if it were a prize, he crawled ahead of me. Smiling and motioning for me to follow him he pushed on, leaving behind a thin slippery trail of blood from the headless body of Cain.

I was flabbergasted.

I was thankful.

I was scared and crying tears of joyful sadness, but I was still alive.

Barely able to make out the small dark form of Nathaniel's body in front of me, I kept within a few steps of his burlap robe. Crawling with agonizing pain, I found myself following more by the scratchy sound of the robe, than by sight. We snaked our way through the dusty vents, stopping only occasionally to catch our breath. Trudging on we came to a T shaped intersection that was dimly lit by the light of a room that shined through the aluminum vent cover. As I crawled closer to the light, I could see Nathaniel's frail body as he squatted upright upon his squarely planted feet, seemingly ready to dart in any direction. Resting his shadowy figure just out of the stripes of light that escaped from the well-lit room below, he waited. Pulling myself closer to the vent, I looked up and stopped dead in my tracks. Across the stream of light that fell inside the shaft came a thin moving shadow. Someone was down there. I felt my pulse quicken and my heart began to pound harder and louder until it filled my ears with deafening fear. I was a nervous wreck, but I had to look into the room. With the stealth of a cat, I quietly pulled myself within eye shot of the room below. Afraid to look but even more afraid not to, I leaned forward to get a better view. The room seemed familiar but I couldn't quite remember why. It was sterile and spotless and carried the strong odor of alcohol or maybe formaldehyde in the air. From my vantage point, I could see the shadow of a standing figure, as it moved from the left to the right its shadow moved with it. Out of my immediate view, I pulled myself to my knees to try to get a better view. I could barely see the end of a metal table, just like the ones that I had seen before in the catacombs. Also like those other metal tables I could see the feet of a body that rest on top. The feet were small but appeared healthy, and if it weren't for the bright green toe tag, I would have assumed that these were the feet of a healthy person that was very much still alive. With eyes once glued to the base of the feet, I felt them begin to move slowly up to the ankles. Around the ankle was a gold chain with a connecting charm, it was too far to make out its exact shape and design, but it somehow looked familiar. Following up her leg to the top of one calf I noticed the angle of which it was laying. Her left and right legs were upright but at the same time slanted outward in a way that made the legs appear to have been removed from the body and placed there. Either that or she had to have her legs up, open and pinned to the table. Pondering that thought for a moment, I felt myself freeze in place.

As the sound of footsteps woke me from my trance, I pulled my face from the view bellow. The dancing shadow had returned. As it passed by the vent I got the most eerie feeling that we were being watched, or at least that someone knew we were here in this ventilation shaft. Not daring to move I felt a trickle of sweat begin to fall from my face, landing in a small pool of perspiration that I hadn't noticed before. As the shadow moved, I heard the squeal of the wheels on the bottoms of the steel tables, the body was being moved. Feeling my chest swell with morbid anxiety, I pulled myself closer to the vent, easing my way up only by centimeters at a time. Finally my eyes lay upon the terribly sickening sight of a white female whose body had been split in two, held together only by the spine. Her skin was pulled back exposing her bare flesh, as it was tacked through the small eye of a steel hook that was attached to the inside borders of the stainless steel tables. With about ten or so of these hooks, most of her torso was completely exposed.

128

Giving a clear look at her stomach, intestines and assorted discarded tissue, as most of her organs were already gone. Except for the few that remained in trays on the side of the body, she had been cleanly gutted, much like a fish. Also like a fish, the head had been cut completely off of the body. The cut was quite clean, not jagged fine like you would slice a side of beef. Her arms were also missing and it was clear that her reproductive organs had been looted as well. With her legs pulled up, open and just as I suspected, pinned flat along the sides of the split torso, she looked like a giant frog lying in wait for second period anatomy class. The thought of Christine soon filled my head, I couldn't be sure that this wasn't her. Soon after, my thoughts turned to Red. And then I thought, *her skin was possibly too white to be Christine's, these remains could very well be Red's.* Saddened by the probability that Red was most likely dead, I silently wondered if she really was a cop sent here to investigate the hospital. If that is so then maybe I still have a chance after all. Someone would know of her being here and they'd send help I'm sure or at least I'd like to believe they would. Speculation can't help me now, so I must move on, I must find a way out of this labyrinth of madness. Slowly I began to crawl past the metal vent cover, in route to Nathaniel's position. When suddenly I heard a shout, "Who's there, is some one up there?" shouted the man from inside the room. Totally petrified, I stopped in mid crawl. Barely willing to breath, I held my breath as the voice rang out again, "I said who's there." Before I knew it Nathaniel had snaked his way back to the vent, past my clumsy feet. Placing the index finger of his left hand to his lips, he grouped in the darkness with his right hand. Grabbing a firm grip around the lifeless body of the dead rat, he slammed the tail end of it against the vent. Dragging its tail outside of the vent, exposing it to the room, he wiggled the body for signs of life and then quickly pulled it away from the vent. "Damned rats," exclaimed the voice from the room, following with, "It's getting so they damn near outnumber us." With that he continued on about his gruesome task, turning on an electric saw. Under the cover of the loud buzzing of the saw, Nathaniel and I quickly but quietly slipped away.

We pushed on for what must have been close to an hour. My arms and legs were scraped raw, as the friction burns seared through my pants, eventually burning broad areas of my skin. As we continued to sliver our way through this maze of sheet medal, I was suddenly hit with a cool gush of wind. At that point, I could feel the metal floor beneath me become colder with every step. Feeling that familiar undercurrent of anxiety and fear begin to build, I found myself moving ever so slowly. Inching my way closer to Nathaniel's position, I felt the air begin to stiffen. As I came even closer, I began to make out the familiar bars of yet another vent cover. Wrapping his little fingers around the bars, Nathaniel pushed at the cover with all his might. With a weak scream from the metal as it scraped against the lip of the air duct, the vent cover was soon completely free. Pulling the cover into the air conditioning duct, Nathaniel carefully placed it against the wall. Motioning to me to come on, he quickly made his way down into the source of the increasingly frigid air. Following close behind him, I began to snake my way out of the duct and into what looked and felt like a cold storage warehouse. But before I could get past my waist, I felt the full palm of Nathaniel's hand come crashing down on the back of my head.

What the hell did you do that for? I yelled.

"Oa ate, oa ate," he whispered.

Turning my head to see his lips in the dim lighting, I watched as his lips pronounced, "The gate, up there, get the gate," this he mouthed as he pointed into the shaft that I was still hanging from. Knowing now that I needed to somehow back into this vent and retrieve the cover, I tried unsuccess-fully, failing on my first two attempts. Finally, I mustered up enough strength to wrangle my way back into the air duct. After passing the cover to Nathaniel, I crawled out of the duct until gravity stepped in and forced me to drop to the ground, head first. With outstretched arms, I reached for the ground to break my fall. As I tumbled head over feet, I managed to fall without hurting myself at all, with the exception of a little pain from some of my previous wounds. Flat on my back, I laid there looking straight up at the dark ceiling. Soon after, I felt the nagging grip of the ice cold floor begin to rob my body of its precious heat. Making my way back to my feet for the first time in hours, I cautiously walked over to where the vent cover was lying. Picking it up, I carefully placed it back into the wall above my head. The air was so cold that clouds of white smoke billowed from my mouth every time I exhaled. Nathaniel was nowhere in sight. Unable to see beyond the tips of my fingers, I walked slowly into the darkness whispering Nathaniel's name. *Nathaniel, where are you?* There was no reply. Taking small and calculated steps, I groped in the darkness with open palms. Blindly searching for signs of life, I felt even for walls or anything that would help me along. Feeling a terrible anxiety begin to swell in my gut, I tried to call out to Nathaniel once again, and again there was no reply. *Something must be terribly wrong,* I thought, *surely he would have answered by now if he could have.* Not knowing what to do next, I continued to grope my way through the darkness. Suddenly without warning, I heard the click of a light switch. Instantly, I could see. What I saw made me tremble with unshakable fear. Panning from left to right, I saw the frozen remains of dozens of bodies, some with their heads and some without. They were piled up on top of one another, thrown in corners and scaling each wall as far as I could see. The bodies were unclothed and most of them seemed somehow hollow, as they were bent and twisted like rag dolls. It was one of the most sickening sights that I have ever seen. In one pile there were nothing but limbs, arms and legs, and even a few fingers. In another pile were torso's with protruding rib bones that gave way to vacant cavities of emptiness. Emptiness, where there once were life sustaining vital organs. Frozen tears now stuck to my face as I came across a head without a body, it was loosely wrapped in a blue knitted garment. With the hair still in tack, fiery red that it was, and the familiar blue shawl, I soon realized the sickening truth, it was Red. Falling to my knees and bursting into tears I cried aloud without regard to whoever it was that flicked on the lights. Almost completely taken over with madness, I reached out and picked up the head, pulling it close to my chest. With my heart full of anguish and despair, I cradled the head as if it were a new born baby. Her expressionless face told no tale of her horrible demise. With open eyes and a blank stare she looked as if she never knew she had been killed. Unable to move, I knelt there with this frozen head in my arms, frozen tears on my face and not a clear thought in the forefront of my mind. I was gone, totally transparent. Not able to interpret the madness any longer, I remained on my knees until a dark hooded Nathaniel returned to wake me from my petrified state. Crouching down beside me he reached up to remove his hood. Still on his feet but bending both knees, he looked deep into my eyes with the compassion and understanding that vastly exceeded his years. Without saying a word, he reached out to take the frozen head from my arms, first wrapping it with the blue knitted shawl. Cradling Red's head just as I had, he walked over to a pile of frozen bodies and carefully placed the head on top. Walking back over to my position, he pulled his hood up over his head, bent down and took my hand in his. Pulling at my hand to tell me that it was time to go, he squeezed and tugged while gesturing with his free hand. I picked myself off of the freezing floor, stood up straight on my cold bare feet, and took in a deep breath of the crisp, dry air. Without looking back and without uttering a sound, Nathaniel led the way with me in tow, as we cautiously strolled into the mystery of the billowing white fog.....

Chapter 14

"The Chase"

It seemed the shaft had led us into a back room within the morgue. As we made our way through the white mist, it soon gave way to a long corridor that seemed to be littered with frozen debris As I followed Nathaniel's small frame through the cluttered mess in our path, I got the distinct feeling that he was quite at home here. Amidst the scores of bodies and frozen body parts, this ten year old child had grown accustomed as if it were perfectly normal. Negotiating our way through one room after another, Nathaniel silently led the way through this morbidly chilling tomb. Hardly able to feel my frozen feet, I tripped and fell hard. Tumbling and rolling a few paces, I slid on the ice slicked floor until I was eventually stopped by a pile of bodies. Taking a moment to catch my breath, I inhaled deeply. Gagging on the frigid air as it hit the back of my throat, I struggled to breathe. Perhaps now aware of my temporary demise, the sound of Nathaniel's small bare feet smacked the floor of this frozen ice box. As he quickly made his way over to me, he lashed out to my seated position clamping his small curled palm against my mouth. "Shhhh," he said as he stood up and listened for the slightest of sounds.

Trying desperately to comply, I soon lost control of my frozen windpipe and my throat erupted as I tried frantically to breathe normally. Badly coughing and wheezing, I felt as if I had a garden hose caught in my throat. I struggled to get a grip of myself, but it was obviously too late. Out in the distance rang, "Over here, I hear something over here, hurry." Now too terrified to think straight, I looked to Nathaniel for our next move. He pointed in the direction of the door. Before I could be sure of the plan, he raised his right hand baring his little fingers. He raised a first, then a second finger and finally a third, with that he sprinted ahead for the door. Needing no explanation, I jumped to my feet and ran as fast as my legs would carry me. Shouts from all sides rang out, "There he is, get him." I ran with all that I had left in my body, not looking in any direction but forward. Nathaniel had already made it to the great door and he looked as if he were trying to close it shut. Making it just in time I squeezed my way through to the other side. With no time to spare, we pushed the giant door closed. After tightly securing the heavy latch, we quickly dropped in the steel pin. Coughing and wheezing still, though with relief, I fell listlessly to the floor. Now up against the wall, I clutched my chest as it continued to tighten from complete exhaustion. With Nathaniel now bending on one knee at my side, I sat with my head between my legs. Suddenly, the loud and angry pounding from inside of the morgue broke the silence. They must have been right behind me. That's why Nathaniel was going to close the door even on me. It seems if I had taken just ten seconds longer I'd be dead. *What a strange thing it is indeed to learn such hard, cold lessons from a ten year old,* I thought.

Faintly, I could hear through the door, "You'll never get out alive," as the pounding continued. Making it to my feet, I spun around with the realization that I had been here before. This was the very spot that Red saved me. This is the meat locker that I was being wheeled into before Red saw my eyes blink. Motioning for me to follow, Nathaniel led me into the room where at one time, I was left to die. We were standing directly in the heart of what the nurses affectionately called, "The Pre-Morgue." For the first time I realized just how large the room was. There were at least two dozen occupied gurneys, all of the occupants were presumably expected to die soon. As soon as they would expire their bodies would no doubt be plundered and looted of its rich organs and tissues. Each body was hooked up to a battery of electrodes, monitors and intravenous feeding tubes. Curiously enough, I hadn't seen these things when I was last here; I guess they learned something since my case. Maybe they realized they needed stricter controls, after all letting the souls liberate themselves without direct supervision could damage the organs. I wished there was something that I could have done, but honestly all I could think about was getting far away from the hospital, far away from this unending nightmare. Although the need for self preservation was strong, I couldn't help but feel sympathy for these trapped souls. They're here just as I once was, but as fate would have it, I was still fighting and running for my life, and they were still waiting for theirs to be snatched quietly in the solitude of this reserved parlor of death; the room where screams go unheard, tears fall un-wiped, and souls are snatched from broken bodies doomed for cannibalizing dismemberment. All of this in the name of hate; fear and profit.

The pressure was mounting and it was clear that Dr. Michael's henchmen were fast on our trail. It wouldn't be long before someone heard the banging on the morgue door, and I was sure they'd be plenty mad at us for locking them inside. Not planning on waiting around for that, Nathaniel and I made our way through the long corridor back past the huge door, where they continued to pound away from inside. As we approached the elevators, the doors shockingly began to open. Quickly, we darted towards the stairs. Just as we made it to the door, I heard the rumblings of voices and the clang of shoes as they made contact with the cement stairs. Now trapped between the elevator and the stairs, we had about five seconds to decide what to do. Should we run back to the room of sleepers, stand and take our chances with the elevator, or wait in the stairwell in which case we'd surely be caught. Before I could completely assess my options, Nathaniel grabbed my hand and pulled me into the stairwell. With only seconds to spare, he quietly pushed the door closed behind us and shot like a light under the winding staircase that spiraled its way upward. Joining him in this tiny crawl space under the cement stairs, we waited in silent terror. If we would have waited two seconds more, we would have been caught. By the sound of the footsteps, I estimated the gang to be perhaps a half dozen. One by one they raced to the bottom of the stairs, striking the closing door before it had a chance to close completely. As they scuffled down the hall, I could hear them as they greeted the occupants of the elevator, "down here, they're locked inside the freezer." Overhearing the squeals of a walkie-talkie, but not able to make out what was being said, I knew they would not rest until they found us. I knew for sure, we were doomed. Meanwhile, with nerves of steel, Nathaniel sat there expressionless, legs crossed, and hands clasped together with interlocking fingers. And just like a good poker player he waited perhaps another twenty seconds. A good thing too, there were two more stragglers that came racing down the stairs and through the door. Seconds after they made their way down the hallway, he leaped to his feet and motioned for me to follow. In no time we ran up two flights of steps, stopping cautiously at the exit door. He opened the door a bit and peeked onto the floor. Opening the door further to signal that all was clear, we quickly dashed past a few patients' rooms and finally made our way to the linen closet. The room that doubled as a janitor's closet was truly the gateway to hell.

This time I knew not to go racing through the secret passage. Remembered the terrible fall I took the last time I was there, I was much more cautious. Following Nathaniel's lead I quietly and carefully made my way down the slippery staircase. Before making it to the bottom of the stairs he jumped over the side and called for me to do the same. Barely able to see him at this point, I followed almost exclusively by sound. Feeling the soft cool earth beneath my feet, I knew we were headed for the catacombs. I continued to follow Nathaniel, although I struggled with mixed emotions. I owe him my life and of course I'm grateful for his rescue. However, I continue to agonize over the thought that I've lived through another day only to die another death tomorrow. *I am 'Dante,'* I thought, *and this is my inferno.* Death it seemed is as slippery, dark and dangerous as is life. I continued to wonder if I were dead. Continuously, I wondered if I was to go on into perpetuity almost meeting my demise, escaping only by the skin of my teeth. *No matter*, I thought, *I have no choice but to go on, I have to continue to play the game.*

This was the worst, most horrifying game that I've ever had to play in my life, or was it my death? I suppose you could say I've been playing a mean game against the devil; that it was hard to tell exactly who was winning. Sadly, the sickening pain in the pit of my gut told me that I would probably be the loser in the end.....

Chapter 15

"Christine"

Now completely exhausted, Nathaniel and I began to slow our brisk gait down to a steady jog, then to a slow walk and finally down to standing still in our tracks, ankle deep in a mixture of soil and sand. Bending over to catch my breath, I felt a severe burning sensation in my left kidney, reminding me that I haven't had water in days. I was quite surprised to see that Nathaniel even had to catch his breath, something that I had never seen up until now. As we took a moment to compose ourselves, neither of us spoke a word. The pain in my kidney began to subside as I laid down flat on my back. Lying against the cool earth, I stared out into the familiar orange glow, presumably from torches in the wall just up ahead. Desperately I tried to make sense of my plight, but that battle was lost before it began. Tears began streaming down my face as I once again made the mistake of accepting my reality in all its horror and all of its accompanying pain. I then pulled my knees up to my chest, transforming my body into the fetal position. While tightening myself into this position I began brushing the dirt and debris from my arms and legs. It was then that I realized my feet were covered with seething blisters. Most of the blisters were swollen with fluid and some had already erupted. As the liquid continued to ooze from my new wounds, I began to notice for the first time, a dull but constant stinging on the soles of my feet. Finding a pointed twig in the sand I began to work on my feet. With the sharp edge I punctured the swollen blisters one at a time, relieving them of the pressurized fluid that squirted freely as I pricked the tough skin. The pain was only slight until I tried to put my full weight back on my feet. Hardly able to stand, I fell crashing to the ground as the pain was greater than I expected. Worried about how I was to go on I felt the pangs of fear and uncertainty begin to pull at my insides. Looking out in all directions I had to all but cover my mouth to prevent myself from screaming at the top of my lungs. The frustration was mounting as I broke out in a cold sweat. Having witnessed the beginnings of my nervous breakdown, Nathaniel came over to where I was now seated and placed his small hand on my shoulder. In his own sweet but garbled voice he said, "It'll be ok." After giving me several reassuring pats on my shoulder and back he turned and began to walk away. Looking up at his shadowy frame, I noticed him taking slow and methodical steps with his head down as if he was looking for something. Finally he stopped about ten paces from me on my right. With his back still turned he looked back at me once and then proceeded to urinate onto the ground beneath him. Thinking that a little odd, at least the way that he went about it, I shook my head and turned my eyes back to the dark ceiling. When I no longer heard the splashing of his relieving himself, I turned my eyes back to his position and again his actions took me by surprise. Without moving a step he squatted with his chest against his knees and looked down as if to inspect the spot that he had just urinated in. Then curiously with both open hands he stabbed the very spot. Working his hands further into the urine soaked dirt, he scooped up as much as his little hands could carry, turned and began to walk in my direction. Having no idea what to expect next, I just watched and waited for him to reach me. When he came within inches of my feet he dropped to his knees and separated his hands into two fists full of dark wet earth. To my amazement he began to smear the mixture onto the soles of my feet. Almost immediately my feet stopped stinging as he spread the pasty earth over the entirety of both feet top and bottom.

"Better?" he asked.

With a bright warm smile I replied, *Yes Nathaniel, much better, thank you.*

Wiping the dirt from his hands on his robe, he crawled up next to me and put his arms around my waist. After squeezing in a quick but tight hug, he then buried his hooded head into my chest. Placing my arms around him as if holding for dear life, I gently rocked him from side to side in an effort to restore some semblance of hope. As he sobbed ever so softly in my arms, I felt the tears begin to swell in my eyes until their lids could no longer carry the load. And together, arm in arm we quietly cried ourselves to sleep.

Not long into a soothing dream of better days and better times, I was abruptly awakened by the not too distant sound of a commotion and the muffled screams of what sounded like a woman. Still quite exhausted, I felt my eyelids flutter to a close. Suddenly the noise began again. My eyes sprung open, and like a cat, Nathaniel leaped to his feet. This time the sound was louder and it seemed to be coming from just up ahead, a few feet into another chamber. Before I could make it to my feet, Nathaniel had already started in that direction to investigate. As I stood I noticed the pain in my feet was gone and I was again ready for travel. In the dim orange glow I could just about make out the dark hooded form of the boy. Gingerly placing one foot in front of the other, in anticipation of the inevitable pain, I walked toward him. Strangely enough, there was no pain at all. As I made my way over to the little guy, I looked on while he steadily brushed away at what looked like a normal pile of dirt and debris, seemingly no different from any of the other piles that littered the cavern floor. Not far into the dig, his efforts were eventually rewarded. At the base of the pile was a flat surface that was different from the cavern wall. Using his finger nails he scraped the surface a bit more, revealing to us a small glass window. Still not able to see through the glass, he stopped abruptly as the thumps became even louder. That, coupled with the stinging sounds of slaps and heavy breathing left us both still and completely silent. This small window was a window to a room of some kind and it seemed someone was either being beaten or having very rough sex in it below. After hearing a series of short terse screams in a females' voice, we heard several loud thumps against the wall. Soon after, the agonizing sounds of a man's voice screaming in pain literally filled the room below. After the screaming stopped, there was a gasping sound coming from what sounded like the raspy voice of a man, then a crashing thud it seemed to the floor. Finally there was nothing but silence. Still unsure of what I just heard, I picked up where Nathaniel left off. Clearing the small window of the hardened dirt that covered it, I spit a little saliva on the glass and eked out a tiny spot of clean glass. Almost touching the glass with one eye I peered into the dimly lit room below. The walls looked as though they were padded, as they were quite dark and bulging. There was a tiny metal bed with a badly stained mattress with no linen on it. As my eye panned left to right I could barely make out a dark form that seemed to be shivering in the farthest corner of the room. Not able to make out much else, I decided to try to clear the window for a better view. As I began to clear more and more of the stuck on debris I pushed a little harder than I had expected on the bottom of the glass and the whole thing began to move inward. Startled by this I jumped back to see if I had broken it, while at the same time readying myself for a quick get away if necessary. The window it turns out was connected to two flat bars on each side that allowed the window to slide open from top to bottom. Terribly afraid to look in but even more afraid not to, I stepped back up to the window and pulled it open as far as it would go. Leaning forward, putting my face into the now open window area, I looked in and down and almost lost it. On the floor was the blood soaked form of a man's body. He was on his back and lying in a pool of blood. His white trousers were half off his body down around his ankles, so too was his underwear. His penis it seemed had been ripped from his body and what remained of it was stuffed into his mouth. Stunned by such a gruesome sight I had hardly noticed the whimpering form in the corner. It was a woman as I had suspected. She was mostly naked with scraps of fabric sparsely covering her body. Bruises covered her legs and arms as I could hardly see much else as she tried desperately to cover herself. At that moment a flash of light went streaming past my eyes, only it was my mind that created this light. The flash of light was really a flashback to the awful scenes that landed me in this terrible place to begin with. In a matter of seconds I relived the horrible terror that I felt when my precious Christine was being brutalized and there was nothing I could do about it. I remembered the sense of helplessness and hopelessness. Turning my eyes briefly from the scene below, I found it hard to hold back the tears as the images continued to tear at me without mercy. Despair is the ever present cloak that I wear and it's as familiar to me as my name. Dazed and stuck in the dreadful memories of the past, I could hardly move. Awakened from my paralyzed state by the rumbling in the room below, I looked up to see a sight that would put me in a complete state of shock. The still whimpering woman below was now looking straight up at me. With her arms reaching out toward me, blood on her mouth and hands, and all over her face. Her dark hair was matted and all over her face as well. She was trying to call out to me but I couldn't make out what she was trying to say. *My God, it can't be, it just can't be,* I screamed aloud. *Christy, I screamed, is that you?, is it really you? Oh God, oh God, Christy please let me see you, is it really you?* Thrusting my arm through the open window, *Christy, please if you are my Christy please come to me, please.* Rising to her feet she moved closer to the window and in better light. It was my Christine and I was floored. My insides turned to jelly and I didn't know what to do. I couldn't believe it, yet there she was, in this insane hospital all the time. As she moved closer, she turned her face away while wiping the blood from her mouth. Coming steadily closer there was no mistake, trapped in this padded cell all this time was the one person that I loved more than life itself. The emotions that flooded my body and mind were too much to interpret. I couldn't think. I couldn't act. I could only cry as I looked deep into the eyes of my beloved, the horrors she must have been through, was all that I could think of. The pain and sorrow in her eyes broke my heart into a thousand pieces and again I found myself dangling on the verge of a nervous breakdown. My body was cold, my mind was numb and what was left of my spirit was now completely hollowed.

With my arm still dangling through the window, I sat dazed as the tears wouldn't stop streaming down my face, when I felt the warm touch of the tips of Christine's fingers.

The mere touch of my lost love was enough to breath new life into my dying body; with her touch came new possibility. *Maybe I can lick this thing,* I thought, *maybe I will survive after all.* Turning my attention now to getting her out of this cell, I planned to test the strength of this small window. Pulling on it as hard as I could did absolutely nothing. The window was solidly fastened to the metal frame and after taking a better look, I'd determined she'd never fit through any way, even if I could pull the window ledge out completely. The window was only five inches or so high and about a foot wide. Pacing back and forth I wracked my brain trying desperately to think of a way to free her. Suddenly in the distance I heard the squeal of a walkie-talkie and the chatter of guards who were hot on our trail. *They must be following our foot prints,* I thought. Faced with a hell of a dilemma, I searched every fiber of my being for the answer, but nothing came. If I stayed I'd surely be captured, but how could I leave her now that I know she's alive. Nathaniel pulled on my arm saying, "Go, got to go."

I can't leave her Nathaniel, she's my wife, I can't go without her, I explained.

"Go now, hide, come back, ok?" he said in his garbled soft voice.

As I dropped to my knees to close the glass, Christine screamed and begged me not to leave her. I told her I needed to hide, that the guards were chasing me and I'd come back for her. She screamed even louder and pleaded with me not to leave her. It was then that I noticed that she talked in the same manner as Nathaniel. *Christy I can't understand you, I said, do you understand?* I asked. With that she stepped back away from the wall so I could see her. She then opened her mouth, while erupting in tears she revealed that she too had her tongue cut out. Shaking my head in disbelief, I assured her that I was going to hide just until the guards passed, that she should remain very quiet until I returned. *Can you do that for me Christy?* I asked.

She shook her head yes and sat back on the floor in the furthest corner from the window. With the guards closing fast, I resealed the portal shut. First closing the window tightly then covering it again with the dirt and debris. By then Nathaniel had already begun to smooth over our tracks. Now on his hands and knees he gestured for me to do the same. As there seemed to be endless tunnels in these catacombs, we made our way back to the entrance of the one we had strayed into. Having backed out of the tunnel while smoothing over our tracks, we rejoined our previous tracks leading instead into a different tunnel. This one already had many tracks in the sandy dirt and we hoped they'd follow them to where ever they lead. Stopping in mid step, Nathaniel jumped off to his left, rolling for a few yards eventually making his way to a large drainage pipe that was well hidden in the dark amidst the clutter of the dark sand. Following his lead I did the same, making my way to this drainage pipe. Through the pipe we crawled, in silence and complete darkness. After crawling for about fifteen minutes we stopped. There we waited and still no words were spoken.

Finally Nathaniel turned and said, "We stay here, they'll stop looking."

Will they ever stop looking? I asked.

"They'll think the crazies got us," he said.

The crazies! Who? What are the crazies? I asked.

Before I got an answer he was fast asleep. *As if we didn't have enough problems, I find myself now faced with the crazies, whoever or whatever they are,* I thought. Fearful for more than just a few moments my thoughts soon returned to Christine. For the first time in a long time, I actually felt optimistic. I could even smile again, as the prospects of freedom and life with my beloved Christine seemed possible again. Warmed by these thoughts, I gently closed my eyes, no longer able to stop myself from falling prey to the pressing need for sleep....

Chapter 16

"The Crazies"

Abruptly, I was awakened by the pounding fists of a fiercely agitated Nathaniel. Pulling on my ragged shirt collar he cried, "The Crazies, the crazies, they're coming, they'll eat us if they catch us." Barely able to understand him, the sound of stark terror in his voice was easily enough to get my attention. Still partly asleep, I began to hear the distant echo of animal like sounds resonating throughout the storm drain. Now quite alarmed, I jumped to my feet. With bent knees, I ran as fast as I could behind the quick footed and distancing sound of a terrified Nathaniel. As my back scraped along the ceiling of the drain, the pounding in my chest grew stronger. The snorting, squealing and wheezing sounds of the crazies, grew louder and seemed to get closer as I ran harder and faster. Nathaniel was nowhere in sight and I could no longer hear his voice guide me as to which way to go. This was particularly troubling because I was approaching a fork in my path. With just a faint hint of light I could see that the piping began to split into two directions. One bent off to the left and the other continued on, with a slight curvature to the right. Not knowing which way to turn, I continued to awkwardly run and crawl as swiftly as I could through the straighter opening that curved to the right. The storm drain was now pitched black and the wild boar-like sounds filled the air. Out of my mind with fear and panic, I didn't dare stop even though my side ached terribly from the steady run.

My long steady strides became shorter, my breathing became heavier and cramps began to seize my stomach, tying it into knots. The sounds were stifling and growing even louder. The crazies knew exactly which direction I took and they were right behind me, hot on my trail. *They must be able to smell me,* I thought. No longer able to contain my fear, I began yelling for help, as I braced myself for a horrible end. Now on my hands and knees, I continued to crawl through the drain, finally making my way to the end of the pipe that was capped with metal bars. Staring through the bars into the burnt orange glow of a distant torch, I screamed for help, pleading to be rescued by anyone. Anything, I thought was better than meeting up with whatever it was that was making such God-awful sounds. Even the orderlies would be a welcomed sight right about now. Firmly gripping the bars with both hands, I shook as hard as I could, but the metal barred cover didn't even budge. The creatures were now so close that I could smell them, and it sounded as if there was a lot of them. The smell was overpowering; like a herd of buffalo. Trapped like an animal, I surveyed my situation and stopped screaming. Putting my back up against the bars while gripping them with both hands, I prepared to use my legs as weapons. *Anything to keep these creatures off of me,* screamed in my mind. Bracing myself, I took a deep breath, professed my love for Christine and asked God to please make my death a swift one. Then suddenly without warning I began falling backward, as the gate swung free crashing against the outside wall.

"Hurry, I can see them, there coming, hurry up— get out," screamed the familiar voice of Nathaniel. As I backed out of the storm drain I fell down to the familiar dirt floor of the catacombs. Before I knew what was happening, he had lifted the heavy gate in an effort to reseal the opening of the storm drain. Quickly regaining my senses, I helped him close the gate. As I pushed it all the way into place, he quickly jumped on top of the protruding pipe. With just seconds to spare, he quickly replaced the little piece of metal that kept the gate in place. As soon as he made it back down to the dirt floor, a pair of badly mangled human hands wildly tugged at the bars, while others soon tried to reach through. Apparently frustrated by the loss of a meal, one of the creatures became even more violent, slamming his head into the bars over and over again, in a futile attempt to break through. In the dim light, I could see the hideous face of what looked barely human. Its teeth were almost fully exposed, with no lips. It had no nose to speak of. Neither did it have ears and lacked most human facial features. Between patches of hair were the deep scars that went from one side of their head to the other. Some even had what looked like surgically stitched scars that went from the top of their heads to the bridge of what once was a nose. With blood shot eyes that stared through you, appearing as if they belonged to the devil himself, they stared me down. Realizing once again that I had narrowly escaped death, I sat in silent disbelief. My mind was reeling and my heart was pounding as if it was trying to jump out of my chest. As I began to look around, I felt a strange sense of familiarity.

Have we been here before, I asked Nathaniel.

He shook his head yes and pointed to a wall with a mound of sandy dirt pushed up against it. In a strange twist of fate, we ended right back in front of the window that led to where Christine was being held. Knowing this may be my last chance at saving her I raced over to the mound and began digging. Oddly enough the crazies had vanished from the drain pipe and with that came a limited sense of security, albeit temporary.

"They're coming to get us you know, we have to go, we have to go now," proclaimed the excited kid.

How much time do we have before they get here? I asked.

He responded by shrugging his shoulders and saying, "A few minutes, five minutes, maybe, but."

I interrupted with, *Help me, I have to get Christine, I have to get my wife, I won't leave her this time and I won't let you leave either.*

With that we both began to dig as fast as we could. As I made it to the window, pulling it open and looking in, there she was still huddled in the corner. *Christine, Christine,* I shouted in a whispering voice. She looked up at me and slowly made it to her feet. Putting my face up to the glass I said, *I'm back to get you honey, I told you I would come back for you.* As I pulled at the metal frame I noticed a few cracks in the cement surrounding it. The air was quite moist and so was the ground, which led me to believe that the nearby ocean probably floods the catacombs from time to time. If that is the case it was likely that the stone wall would give way if I pulled at the frame hard enough. I pulled and pulled with all my might as the frame began to loosen, just slightly. Realizing my time was running out, I told Christine to move away from the window, that I was going to attempt to kick it in. I then closed the window and began kicking at the frame and the surrounding cement. Blow after blow, I kicked with all my might, directly on and around the window. "They're coming, they're coming, we got to go, I don't want to get eaten," screamed Nathaniel. I could barely hear them so I estimated I had another few minutes. Feverishly I kicked and pounded on the crumbling cement. Finally it began to give way. I kicked and kicked and kicked some more until, finally the glass and frame went flying into the room below. Now with the hole in the wall just a little larger than the frame I began to chip away at it until it was large enough to reach in and pull Christine to freedom. By now, the crazies were little more than two minutes from where we were. Hoping the hole was large enough; I reached in with both arms and beckoned for Christine to grab *hold.*

We don't have much time, I shouted, grab hold Christine, grab hold.

She was so traumatized she began backing up shaking her head no.

"I can't leave, I'll be punished, I'll be punished," she said over and over.

I won't let them, I said. I won't let them punish you love, I'm here to take you home, ok?

Pulling at my pant leg, Nathaniel pleaded for me to hurry. *Come on honey you can do it, but we have to leave now, the crazies will get you if I leave you and then you would be punished, do you understand?*

Slowly, she began to walk back to the hole in the wall where my arms were waiting for her to grab hold of. Feeling her hands grip both of mine, I grabbed hold and slowly pulled her up through the hole. When I pulled her out completely I could hardly believe that right before me was my beloved Christine. She was my life, my soul mate, my wife. As she stood before me in tears, I dropped to my knees with my arms around her waist as tears of joy splashed off my smiling cheeks and into the sand.

"They're here, the crazies, they're here," exclaimed a terrified Nathaniel.

With the crazies now within sight, I knew I had to come up with something and damn fast. Realizing our only escape would be to make it back to the drainage pipe, I leaped to my feet, grabbing the hands of both Christine and Nathaniel. In no time we made our way back to the metal grate that covered the opening to the drainage pipe. Removing the retaining pin as I'd seen Nathaniel do before, I quickly pried loose the cover and helped Nathaniel in first as Christine was reluctant to go in first, then I helped Christine into the large pipe opening. Hopping into the pipe myself, I quickly turned around to pull up the grate. As I reached down to grab hold of the bars, I leaned out just far enough to see that dozens of the creatures were closing in on us from both sides. As I pulled the grate shut, I realized I didn't have the retaining pin. *Oh God,* I thought, *the only thing that was keeping those things from getting to us was that little piece of metal. Nathaniel do you have the pin, have you seen it?* I practically begged him. We all began to feel around in the dark, when Christine found it under her leg. She handed it to me and I tried to silently reach through the bars and replace the pin which was on top of the outside of the metal grate. *Nathaniel,* I called, *I need you to reach through and put the pin back in the hole.* With his hood off, I could see the absolute terror in his eyes, as he violently shook his head no. And like the child that he was, he grabbed for Christine's waist and held on for dear life. *They're going to get us if you don't do this Nathaniel, my arms are too big to fit through the bars, and we don't have any more time left.* With a slight whimper he let go of Christine's waist, grabbed the pin from my hand and softly walked toward the metal grate. There he slowly reached his tiny hand through the bars, extending his arm up and out, right up to his elbow. Fumbling around for a few seconds, he then smiled and quickly snatched his arm back from harm's way. Knowing those creatures were all around us we didn't dare make a sound. Not moving a muscle, we all huddled together in the hopes that they would just pass by. Suddenly without warning, one of them screeched in a horrible voice as it pulled on the bars with one hand while trying desperately to reach inside with the other. With that, Christine let out a shrill scream, alerting the rest of them that we were still inside the drain. Before you knew it, scores of creatures were swarming around the outside of the bars, pulling and tugging and trying to reach inside to get at us. Before I could decide exactly what to do, the hellish group began to thin. I could hear them rumbling outside, and excitedly squealing, fighting like a pack of wolves. Before long they all had left from in front of the bars. Inching my way back to the bars, I tried to get a look without getting too close to the grate. From my vantage point, I could see the hole in the wall a few yards away, where Christine was being held. The lighting was still very dim, so I wasn't able to see entirely but I knew instantly what had happened. They must have made it into the room below and discovered the body of the orderly. I watched as the gruesome feast diverted all attention from us. One by one they went in and came out with their share of the human carcass. Like cackling hyenas they gorged themselves. Fighting, snatching and running to a solitary spot to enjoy their meal, they all seemed satisfied. Under the cover of their new found feast, I decided not to push our luck any further as we quietly slipped away. Nathaniel was leading the way, Christine was in the middle and I was pulling up the rear. We found that we had once again cheated death out of its bounty. We were able to live through yet one more day, with the truer question being, *how much longer would we last?*

Too exhausted to run, we crawled until we reached the fork in the pipe. This time we went down the drainage opening on the left. Still on our hands and knees, we continued down the clanking shaft until we were met with a small steady stream of water. The strong salty smell told us this was sea water. The water was so cold that we had to get up from our knees and walk in a crouched position with our backs parallel to the top of the drain. As we continued to walk I began to see a small patch of light up ahead, it was still quite far ahead but light has a way of peering through the tiniest of cracks. At that exact moment I began to feel a steady vibration that shook the entire drainage pipe. With that came the oddest rumbling sound, one that I hadn't heard before. Realizing that whatever it was it probably wasn't good, I yelled to Nathaniel to hurry and get us out of here. But before I could get the last word out of my mouth we were all violently washed through this giant metal tube by a forceful wall of sea water. The speed and force of the water shot us through like bullets. With water rushing up my nose and in my mouth, I grabbed a hold of Christine and Nathaniel as we all crashed against each other, as well as the top, bottom and sides of the drainage pipe. We were tossed and turned like blue jeans in a wash cycle. I couldn't see a thing as my eyes were on fire from the salty water. Still holding my breath, I tightly gripped the hand of each of my traveling companions. Just when it seemed my lungs would explode, we were shot out of the giant drainage pipe. Hurling through the air, we would free fall some fifty feet until we crashed into about five feet of water below.

Having smacked the water with violent force, our clinched fist chain was broken and we were all on our own. Hitting my knees on the bottom, I rushed to my feet pushing myself upward in search of air. As I broke the surface of the water I tried to take in as much air as I could, but all I could do was gag and cough and spit out the salty water that had begun to fill my lungs. The stinging in my eyes was so intense, that I still couldn't see. I could still hear however, and one of the sweetest sounds to my ears was the sound of Christine coughing and spitting out the water as I did. Continuously blinking in an effort to restore my vision, I followed the sound of Christine's voice, wading in the chest high water. Making it over to her position, I threw my arms around her, kissing her face as I swept her hair from her eyes.

Are you alright? I asked.

She shook her head yes while continuing to clear her throat of the bitter, salty water. Totally consumed with her plight I all but forgot about Nathaniel. When just around the bend I heard the splash of a playful, water treading Nathaniel. With the excitement of a ten year old, he gave us a huge toothless smile and waved to signal that he was ok. Like a fish in its own element, he ducked under the water and swam over. There, we frolicked and played in the water like children. Our problems though always close, seemed just a little farther behind us now. The reunion was complete. For the moment there was laughter and joy. For the moment, there was happiness....

Chapter 17

"Rays of Hope"

Looking up at the high ceiling, I watched as the glistening reflection of the water danced across its bumpy surface. The fluid lines and shapes drifted to the stone walls as well. It was then that I began to feel a slight breeze, as the temperature of the chest high water seemed to fall dramatically. The cavern began to appear more sinister than it did before, and the laughter and joy that we shared was now nowhere to be found. Our momentary splash of happiness had quickly faded and in its place was now a familiar sense of doom and dread. In this existence, reality is more painful and more ominous than anything that I've ever encountered. As the three of us huddled close together, we stared silently into each others eyes. No doubt we were all asking the same question, "Are we going to make it?" Of course I didn't have an answer, but I wasn't ready to give up trying just yet.

As both Christine and Nathaniel began to shiver, I realized that we had to find dry land. After hoisting Nathaniel onto my shoulders, it seemed best to follow the flow of the soft current. The underground waterway began to narrow as we made our way further down stream. As the current began to pick up speed it also made it just a little easier to walk through the water. The bottom was quite slippery and occasionally my foot would catch the sharp edges of the rocks that lay on the floor of the stream. An eerie quiet filled my ears, broken only occasionally by the distant splash of water that smacked against the sides of the narrowing banks. Walking directly in the middle of the stream we continued on our ill fated journey. As the stream began to twist and bend the echoing sounds of high pitched chirping and fluttering wings filled the cavern. It was just enough to stop us in our tracks. Listening intensely I tried to imagine what could create such sounds. Suddenly without warning we were besieged by thousands of bats. There were so many bats, the ceiling looked like a huge, black, vibrating cloud. Before we could even hope to pass through unnoticed, hundreds of the black winged creatures swooped down to attack our bobbing torsos. Submerging ourselves to escape our attackers we swam under water for a few yards at a time coming up only for air, then immediately ducking back under in an effort to swim to safety. After swimming about a hundred yards or so, we made our way to an indentation in the rocks and stepped out of the water for the first time in hours. The chirping sounds of the bats were still intense, but at least we had escaped their menacing bite. Taking a moment to catch our breath, I couldn't help notice that the high pitched squealing sound continued but it was now accompanied by a sound that was somehow different. Now frantically twitching in every direction, my senses told me that something was not quite right. Before my mind could fully comprehend it, the dark and slimy stone walls began to come alive. Just then, Christine screamed in pain as her feet and legs were covered with a swarm of biting, hungry rats. Before I could free her of the hungry little monsters, I fell to the ground from the weight of the menacing creatures that had began to attack my back and shoulders. The painful pinch of their sharp teeth repeatedly tore into my flesh, leaving me covered in my own blood. Furiously, I fought off the angry rodents, as I jumped back into the water pulling Christine with me. Even under water the fierce rodents continued to tear plugs of flesh from our bodies. Holding our breath we continued to scramble in our frantic attempt to escape the assiduous bites of the tenacious little monsters. After freeing ourselves from the remaining attackers, we looked on as the walls seethed with rats of all sizes. Every tiny crack in the wall must have been a passage way for what looked like tens of thousands of rats. Like lava pouring from the pores of a volcano the rodents dripped and oozed from the honeycombed wall down to the crowded banks that lay below. The three feet wide banks could only accommodate so many of them, thus many of the rats ended up in the water. Scraping and clawing at each other, they scrambled desperately to pull themselves ashore, out of the quickening current of the water.

Still shaken by the ordeal and in obvious pain, Christine dropped her head into my chest and cried aloud. Just a few yards away was Nathaniel treading water with his chin just barely above the surface. Expressionless, he just stared in our direction. It seemed he had jumped back into the water long before we knew just what was happening. Once again he was far ahead of us. I could only imagine what his little eyes had seen since he'd been trapped in this nightmare. His instincts it seemed were to worry about himself first; choosing to help only after his own safety was secured. I supposed that's how he'd survived so long. Ordinarily, I'd adopt the ways that work best, particularly in such extreme circumstances, however things were different in this instance. I couldn't help but feel protective and responsible for both he and Christine. I couldn't help but hope to free us all of this mind bending madness.

My body was on fire. The salty water burned like acid, burrowing deeper into my wounds, eclipsing the original pain from the bites themselves. As the burning sizzled on, I struggled to endure the fire that lay hidden within in the salt. With bats overhead, the walls and banks teaming with rats, we had no choice but to push on through the intense pain. Not able to stop to attend to our wounds, we continued another hundred yards or so. Down stream we came upon another small dry patch of ground that rose from a shallow pool of water off to our left. The smooth rocks on the wall told me it should be safe, not to mention that Nathaniel had taken a moment to rest there himself. Making my way over to the shallows, I followed the stair like rocks up to dry land. Falling first to my knees then on my chest, I turned my head toward the stream. Emerging from the stream was a determined Christine. With a strange look of both anguish and emptiness, she steadily walked in our direction. Curiously enough she had an almost saintly glow about her. Without uttering a word she began to walk up the stone steps. With both arms at her sides, she was about waist high in the water when my eyes fell from her face to both of her clinched fists. In each of her tightly clinched fists, were the lifeless, water-soaked remains of a dead rat; two lost warriors of an army that had once unmercifully attacked us both. As she stepped onto dry land, I could see through the dim light that the rats had done a real job on her legs and feet. By the time she made it over to me, her legs were almost completely covered with blood that poured from dozens of small punctures. She stopped just about a foot from my face as my eyes were fixed on the gaping wounds that oozed of blood from her thighs down to her feet. Then suddenly with a sharp splat, both rats came crashing down on the smooth rocks just inches from my face. In unison they smacked the ground as the tail of the closest one swung across my face. *Shit,* I shouted, as I jumped back against the wall.

As if awakening from a trance, she blinked her eyes a few times and shook her head. Then without warning she screamed a bone chilling scream, dropped to her knees and burst into an uncontrollable fit. Hitting her face and body and clawing at her hair shouting, "get them off, get them off of me." Screaming at the top of her lungs she ripped the remaining rags from her body, completely naked she raced back for the water and jumped in.

"I want them off," she shouted, "help me, they're eating me alive, help me, help me please."

Beginning to cry himself, Nathaniel was quickly on his feet, as he watched the scene unfold. Jumping in after her, I grabbed her arms as she swung them wildly. When I finally got a hold of her, I picked her up in my arms and carried her back to our resting place. Crying hysterically, she shouted, "I want to go home, please take me home, please. This just can't be happening. Why is this happening?" Feeling my eyes swell with tears, I fought hard to choke them back when her body began to tremble uncontrollably. I was reasonably sure she was going into shock. What we had just experienced was bad enough, but to make matters worst the air was quite cool and she was still completely naked. Looking at Nathaniel I said, *she's freezing, we have to warm her up or she'll die right here, right now.* With that he immediately began to take off his black hooded robe. I'd forgotten that he had on clothes underneath. After hand ringing the sopping wet robe, I quickly put it on her, hood and all. Inspecting the rocks for rat holes, I sat upright with my back against the stone wall. With Christine now lying between my legs, I huddled around her body as best I could. Motioning to Nathaniel to lay his body on top of hers, we sandwiched her body in an effort to warm her with the only source of heat that we had our own bodies. With nothing but silence between us, Nathaniel reached out putting his little hand on my neck and shoulder. First looking at his palm then looking up at me, he shoved his opened hand toward my face. "You're bleeding," he said with a familiar tongue-less voice. By then, I was fully able to interpret his speech. As I began to rock both he and Christine, I replied in an exasperated voice, *I know Nathaniel, I know.*

A few hours it seemed had passed and Christine has since stopped shivering. She seemed to be sleeping comfortably and for now she seemed out of immediate danger. Nathaniel was asleep as well, still lying prostrate across Christine. Marveled by the soft, rhythmic movement of the current, I stared long into the pool in search of answers. *What's next?* I wondered. *What's next?* Indeed, this was the prevailing question that one would automatically ask but always hated to."

As my eyes began to wonder around the cavern, I found myself drawn to the intricate patterns that formed on the walls and ceiling from the reflecting light in the water. At that precise moment, I realized that the cavern was much brighter than it had appeared before I fell asleep. With this new found revelation in mind, my eyes probed every crevice in the ceiling and every crack in the walls as well. Then right before my eyes the search ended. Like a sign from God, a once darkened indentation in the rocks began to beam with ever increasing streams of light. The light shined with such intensity that it caused both Christine and Nathaniel to awaken in fear. In a sleepy eyed stupor Nathaniel jumped to his feet, racing to my side. Christine looked up toward the light, sharply turned her fearful stare back in my direction then put her head down on my chest without speaking a word. I didn't know what to think. *Was this heaven opening its gates to us or would I find a gang of awaiting orderlies to be the source behind the light?* I wondered. This was a true reckoning and for the next few minutes, I was paralyzed. Neither of us made a sound and no one moved a muscle. Soon after, it seemed apparent that if it were the work of the orderlies, they would have been all over us by now. If on the other hand it was heaven opening its gates, then surely I was ready to go. Having rationalized through the possibilities, I knew the thing to do was to investigate. As I tried to move Christine, she held on even tighter whispering "Don't go," into my ear.

I must, I replied, gently pushing her off to the side; immediately, she reached for Nathaniel, clutching him tightly to her body. Softly, she cried with dreaded anticipation of what I might find within the light. Soon after making my way over to the light, I realized it was coming from above. As I stepped into the flood of light, I peered up into what could best be described as a chimney-like tunnel going straight up. At first, the light was shining too brightly and I was unable to make out its true source. But soon after, the light grew dim for just a moment; long enough for me to see that the tunnel lead to the outside. The source of light was one that I hadn't seen in a very long time. And when the intensity of the light returned to its former brilliance, I fell to my knees with joy, realizing what I'd found. What I'd found, were the welcoming rays of a bright and warm sun. What I'd found was another reason to hope....

Chapter 18

"Water Soaked"

After scaling the walls of this beaming tunnel, I eventually reached the bars of a metal drainage lid. With both feet firmly planted on opposite sides of the tunnel, I pushed and tussled with the lid in a frantic attempt to shake it loose. In a scraping thud the lid sprung free on one side. Tearing the sticky residue of hardened rust, the lid squealed once more, sprinkling dusty particles into my eyes. With that it broke free. Hearing the metal grate drop to ground above, I pushed onward and upward to find what lie on the other side of this portal. It seemed like a new portal in time. As I made my way to the surface, it felt as if I had been delivered to some kind of "Promised Land." Barely able to contain my euphoria, I excitedly emerged from that other world scrambling for a better view to freedom. With the great sun bearing down on my face, I fell to my knees. I was completely humbled by the powerful ocean that pounded against the face of the cliff. Simultaneously the roaring sea sent the gentlest of waves to curl and flatten and lovingly lap at my feet just before it was recalled back out to sea. Its beauty and majesty were simply overwhelming.

Tucked away at the base of the cliff amidst the jagged rocks was the drainage tunnel. It seemed the watery cavern that was our home for a time was actually water run off for high tide. As the sand was still damp, I assumed that high tide came quite often. The natural formation of the rocks coupled with the strategic placement of the drainage made for a perfect barrier between the hospital grounds and the threat of flooding. Finally realizing that Nathaniel and Christine were not with me, I rushed back to the drain and shouted for them. Responding in no time, they rushed within sight. Now bending from the waist down into the cavern, I extended my arm to meet a skillfully climbing Nathaniel. Scaling the cavern's throat with surprising ease; Christine soon after climbed within reach of my hand and our newly found light of day. And in no time she hurriedly crawled up to the surface, emerging not with a whisper but with a whimper instead.

Breaking into tears she raced to the edge of the small shoreline that lay a few feet from the rocks. Falling softly in the wet sand catching herself with one knee, she shouted at the top of her lungs, "we made it, Goddamn it we made it." Repeatedly she would scream out the same line. With her head lunging out towards the sea, bowing only to the intensity of the sun, she screamed one last time. "Goddamn you, we made it," she screamed. Finally collapsing into the sand, she pounded both clinched fists into the wet stuff, while cursing and teasing the ground beneath her.

Completely overcome with the bitter sweet possibility of victory after all, I rushed to her side. Rolling over on her back, she busted with laughter throwing her arms around my neck.

"We made it," she shouted, "We made it."

Laughing out loud and shouting and smiling from ear to ear, she went on about how we beat them. Then suddenly she turned grim and slowly began to cry. Her soft whimpers soon became torturous screams of agony and pain, in an instant she was out of control. I tried all that I could to console her but truthfully I didn't know if I was doing her much of a favor. It could be that I was setting her up for another let down, particularly since we weren't sure if we had made it at all.

It took some time to get Christine to calm herself down. When she did we even had an opportunity to talk. In a very soft voice she told me of the horrors that took place in the hospital. With all that I had seen, most of what she told me was about things that I hadn't seen or known of before. And before she was finished my heart was ablaze with anger, outrage and deep sorrow. She talked of how the doctors were experimenting with human subjects. How partial brain removal studies were performed on live human beings. She also told me of how the orderlies would routinely rape and beat the female patients. Most she said couldn't scream because their vocal cords were cut. She then added, "It wouldn't have mattered if they could have screamed, it only seemed to excite the bastards even more." We talked for hours, trading bits and pieces of horror stories until we got around to how we thought the other was dead. We cried and talked and cried some more, eventually vowing never to leave each other's side. Meanwhile Nathaniel seemed quite content playing in the water, occasionally staring off into the orange and blue strips of sky that painted the horizon. Indeed the sun was going down, taking with it, its warmth and light. It was at that moment that I began to realize the tide was gently lapping at my legs. Just an hour ago it seemed to be almost twenty feet from where we were sitting. Retreating back to the cover of the rocks, I tried to put the remaining morsels of sunlight to good use. Surveying the land, I walked the small area of dry sand looking up to the top of the cliff. We were in a real fix. The vast ocean was in front of us steadily gobbling up the shoreline; a fifty foot vertical bluff towered behind us and eclipsed both sides as well. As the tide continued to rapidly close on us, the night dropped its cover of darkness even faster. The wind began to pick up, bringing with it thorny little spikes of cold, ocean water that sent chills through to the bones. It was clear that we couldn't possibly scale the perfectly vertical cliff wall, and swimming out to sea would be suicide. If we stayed put, eventually we would be swept out to sea or continually smashed into the rocks as the tide grew in depth and strength. There was only one alternative left. We had to go back down into the cavern and hope that it wouldn't flood as the tide rolls in. Soon the small patch of beach was gone and we were up to our knees with sea water. Quickly we made our way back down the throat of the cavern. Christine headed down first then Nathaniel with me to follow. As we made our way down, trying desperately to cling to the jagged surface without falling, a huge gush of water poured from above. With that we were flushed down the tunnel drain like sewage in a toilet. Crashing into each other we tumbled and spiraled our way down the shaft, smashing against the sharp rocks that lined the slimy throat of the under ground cavern. Finally we splashed across the stone floor from above, stopping just inches from the wet rocky staircase that led to the pulsating stream.

Things quickly turned from bad to worse. By the time we caught our breaths and got our bearings, we soon realized the cavern was doing its job. The cavern was filling with water from the raging sea above. In the dim light I could see that the walls were pouring of water and the stream continued to rise. Again in a fix we looked around for higher ground. Finding higher ground, we sat for a few moments as we watched the bottom of the cavern disappear under the steady climb of the raging water. I was hopeful that our new position would be high enough at twelve feet above last nights' resting place. Rising with amazing speed it continued to climb throughout the night. At one point the water rose within just a couple of feet of overtaking us completely. Eventually, the invading sea water began to level off and the once strong current slowed to a mild flow.

There we sat huddled in a large hole in the rocks. Like the many escaping wet rodents that fought for a dry ledge to life, we continued to cling to ours. Occasionally having to pluck our ledge free of the pesky little invaders, we didn't dare fall asleep. After several hours more of keeping on the alert, I noticed the water had finally begun to fall. And in a blink of a fatigued eye, the water was almost back to its normal level. Climbing down from the ledge we steeped into the ankle high water. Eager to stretch my limbs again, I raced for that familiar passage to freedom— or at least the one that led to the surface. Still unsure of how to escape from above, I thought it would be our best hope. After making it back to the surface, I saw that the tide hadn't completely receded and the tiny beach from the day before was now under about two to three feet of water. The water was calm and the sky was a hazy, bluish gray, while the gentle wind softly caressed my face. Having no intention of returning to the watery grave that lay below, I vowed to find a way out of the mess we were in. Soon, we all had made it back to the surface. As we

stood in the cool water, the sun began to show itself—
pulling the tide back towards its center. In a surprisingly
short period of time the beach had again emerged. Once
again we found ourselves sitting in the dry sand trying to
figure out a way to escape the nightmare. In silence we
stared out toward the sea. Its power was undeniable and
possessed wondrous beauties, but for now it was our captor,
and for that I hated it. This thing had the power to suffocate
the spirit, not to mention every other aspect of one's being. A
clear and present danger was definitely at hand.

   With silence between us we continued to gaze at the
movement of the ocean. The occasional cackle of a sea gull
off in the distance was the only sound that joined the
constant roar of the ocean. Suddenly the crackle of a whip
rang out with an echo. I knew that sound, I felt that whip.
The serpent was back and I was terrified. Soon after I could
just barely hear a man's voice shouting commands of some
sort. And again the menacing sound of that blood thirsty
whip, only this time bringing with it the agonizing screams
of its human target. What emanated from over the ridge was
evil and I started to wonder whether or not to investigate.
Realizing I had little choice in the matter, I prepared myself
for exploration. First telling Christine and Nathaniel to stay
put, I then slowly ventured out into the water. Wading my
way through, I walked straight into the horizon, until my feet
no longer touched bottom. After swimming out some twenty
five yards or so, I reached the farthest corner of the rocky
bluffs edge. As I scaled the jagged wall I quietly made my
way around the bend. Being very careful to stay close to the
base of the bluff, I made my way steadily closer to the shore
line. Pulling myself along the rocks, but mostly swimming
parallel to them, I soon stopped dead in mid stroke. Right
before me was a young black female, completely naked.
Rinsing her body in the salt water, she stood about twenty
feet from where I was treading water. I didn't know her but I
felt that I had somehow seen her before. Her eyes, her eyes
reminded me. She was the girl from the cage, the breeding

grounds. Her eyes were remarkably blank with just a hint of despair. I'll never forget those eyes. Not far from her were several other bathing females. They hadn't seen me I'm almost sure, but I was also sure that she did. About another fifty yards or so up the beach I saw dozens of blacks chained together by the neck and feet. They were chained to each other as if in a 1950's styled chain gang, herded around like cattle just the way they did between the cages in the catacombs. Just the way they did with the slaves of yesteryear. As my blood boiled with rage I also felt a deep sense of hurt and anguish. So cripplingly hollow was the shell of the person that I used to be. I was stunned almost into convulsions, brought back around only by the stern voice of an orderly. Shouting to the girl in front of me and the other bathing females, he roared, "Get your black asses over here." She stared at me with a blank and expressionless face, lifted her hand in a limp goodbye, turned and ran back towards the demanding voices of the two orderlies. Completely beside myself with blind rage and fury, I remained still in the same position, paralyzed and utterly dumbstruck.

Awakening from a brief trance to the crackle of the whip, I soon realized I needed to get back to Christy and Nathaniel. With an even heavier heart than before, I made my way back to the hidden alcove. Dazed and confused by the time I made it to the beach, there I stumbled for a few steps, finally falling with a thud. Face down in the wet sand with my eyes firmly fixed on the curling waves of the ocean, I laid in silence. Still quite mystified, I could almost feel my mind depart from my body, as it aimlessly drifted out to sea. Then suddenly out of the corner of my eye, I spotted a flurry of splashing water accompanied by a set of wildly stroking arms. Christine had apparently swam around the right side of the bluff while I was off to the left. After she made it back to the beach, she collapsed beside me, drawing deep breaths and spitting out salt water.

I asked you to stay here, why did you leave? I shouted, *where did you go anyway? Answer me,* I screamed, as I raised my hand to her in anger.

Flinching and cowering beneath me she burst into tears, balling her body into the fetal position. Realizing what I was about to do, I fell back in the sand, horrified and totally ashamed of myself.

I'm so sorry, I whispered. *Please forgive me, I don't know what came over me but I'd give my life before I let anything happen to you.*

Pulling her close to me, I continued to beg for her forgiveness, but all she could seem to do was cry. No longer able to conceal my pain, I finally broke down and my weakened eyes overflowed with tears. And together we cried and held each other tight, as if to let go was to crumble and die. Locked in our embrace we tried desperately to heal the wounds of our love starved hearts. Feeling safe in her arms I prayed to God that I'd never have to let her go.

Soon after we loosened our embrace and she accepted my apology. She then assured me that she knew I loved her. For the moment I felt just a little more whole, a little more complete. Suddenly with a sense of panic, I leaped to my feet yelling, *Where's the kid? where's Nathaniel?*

"He's alright," she said.

Well, where is he? I questioned, trying to lower my voice.

"We swam around the other side of the bluff, just to see what was over there," she said. "We thought just in case you didn't find a way out, we could look at the same time. When we made it to the other side we heard a few voices so we tried to get in closer. When we finally cleared the rocks the most horrible scene was unfolding. There were dozens and dozens of people cleaning themselves in the water, all of them were naked, and all of them were black, it was horrible. They were mostly men, but there was a huddle of women washing themselves as well. There were even a few couples having sex right where they stood in the water. In the sand stood a very large, dark skinned black man with rubber boots on. As soon as Nathaniel saw the man he started waving and shouting, swimming in his direction. I called after him but he wouldn't listen, he just swam harder. When he made it over to where the man was standing, he raced up to him, jumping into his arms. I thought maybe it was the boy's father, but I had no idea. I didn't know what to do. I didn't want to show myself, but I didn't think I'd be able to make it back here without resting first. Before I knew it Nathaniel was waving for me to come to shore. No doubt he had already told the man that I was out there bobbing against the rocks. Placing his hand up to his brow, the man took a few steps forward and waved for me to join them. I was scared to death but I hoped that since the kid was so fond of him he'd be one of the good guys. After swimming over to where they were, I became even more terrified. All of the men in the water were shackled at the feet. As the man put his hand out to help me out of the water, he made a bowing gesture while telling me his name was Luther. I noticed his arms had deep welts going up and down them. His face was like that of a jackal, mean, hardened and filled with deceit. His eyes were cold as if they looked right through me. He had the look of a predator and I surely felt like his prey. Before I could say anything, Nathaniel had told him about you and how we were trying to escape this hell hole. Immediately, he offered to help, saying he knew how we could escape, that any friend of Nathaniel's was a friend of his. I don't trust him honey, what should we do?" she asked.

What else did he say, exactly? I asked.

"He said it would be too dangerous to try right away because everyone was looking for us, but that in a day or so things might have cooled off a bit. After that he said for me to go and get you, but not to return until right before dark." She added, "then when I called for Nathaniel to join me, he told me that the boy should stay there with him until we returned.

175

I wasn't sure who I was more afraid for, the boy or for us. Honey what are we going to do?" she whispered. "I can sense nothing short of pure evil coming from that man," she scoffed.

I guess we don't have much of a choice, I responded. *For now we wait until it starts to get dark and then we'll have to put some trust in this Luther, not completely but we have to expose ourselves to some degree.*

After filling her in on what I'd found on the other side of the bend, we soon settled down in a quiet embrace. With the tenderness of an angel she pressed her moist lips up to mine, flooding my veins with psychedelic emotions. God was good to me, if only for once more, he's been good to me. He delivered my Christy to me, perhaps but for one time, never to share another tomorrow. But it's so much more than I had yesterday. Further inspired by the heat of the sun and our intense passion, we exploded with feverish memories of our past. Making love like we had no days left on earth, we collided with the power of the heavens. With steady streams of tears, we tried to melt into each other, connecting at the soul. There, we gorged ourselves of the other, thinking of nothing else. Under a bright clear sky our union was finally complete and for a time we were one....

Chapter 19

"Ground Zero"

The sun was going down and the time was now upon us, we would either be taking our exit to freedom or further falling into the spiraling depths of hell. The tide had already overtaken the island and we were just cornering the bluff's edge. Clinging to the rocks we snaked our way around the slippery mass. On the other side was a makeshift campsite with two amber tipped torches that punctuated its center. There was still just a shot of daylight left and as we swam closer the scene began to take on the feel of a dream. So surreal was this bizarre set up of ropes and logs and nets, and steel, as in cages. Flashbacks of being in the cage pelted my mind's eye with bright and fiery images of hot torturous days of beatings, mind games, rape and murder.

Soaking my head in the water, I then shook it hard to snap myself out of that trance. Soon we reached the shallows, we took to our feet. At first there were no signs of life until we came within a few feet of the waters edge. Stepping forward to greet Christine, she was ahead of me, stood a leather-faced, stony figure of a black man. I assumed this was the man Christine spoke of. She was quite right not to trust him. I didn't trust him and he hadn't even said a word. He extended his hand to Christine, saying, "Welcome back." Then looking up in my direction he added, "Good to finally meet the one who got away." Shunning his help, Christine stepped off to the side and reached back in search of my hand. Together we stumbled to reach the dry sand. As I paused, to catch my breath, the man shouted, "Hurry, we need to get inside."

Through a maze of straw huts that soon gave way to an underground cavern, we followed the man they called Luther. Abruptly he stopped dead in his tracks, turned to us and said, "By the way, I'm Luther." With an evil grimace chiseled on his hardened face, he turned back and continued to lead the way. After a series of twists and turns through the damp corridor, it finally opened up into what looked like a giant stable. With straw and red dirt for a floor, and the God awful smell of livestock in the air, I was sure this was a pen for housing farm animals.

What is this place? I asked.

He responded, "This is the launching pad, 'Ground Zero.'"

What exactly is that? I added.

"In due time you'll know all you need to know," he quipped.

Not good enough, I want to know what the hell is happening here.

"You come to me for help, I extend my hand in friendship and now you make demands. I guess it just ain't in you to be grateful."

Not wanting Luther to get wise to my growing suspicion, I responded.

I didn't mean any disrespect, it's just that we've been through a lot, and the nightmare still hasn't ended.

He responded, "Don't sweat it every body down here has a horror story to tell, makes for a rather nasty disposition. Your contemptuous, disrespectful tone is understandable; remember I'm not the one who brought you here. I'm not the one who sentenced you to hell. Because make no mistake this is hell, and you have been sentenced."

Sentenced by whom, and why? I returned.

Walking us into a larger chamber, he responded, "In due time you'll know all you need to know."

The chamber was bursting with bustling forms. Some were wearing dark hooded robes, while some didn't have on very much at all. In the sweltering heat, the sweat just poured off their bodies. Glistening at every passing of a burning torch, their dark clammy skin shined like beacons in the night. Never speaking a word, they seemed to communicated through gestures and groans. Bending down on one knee to speak to the boy, I asked, *Are these the people that you told me about, you know, the ones that would come and go?* Innocently he clapped his hands together and smiled as he vigorously shook his head up and down. Growing even more impatient with this charade, I just came out with what I really wanted to know.

So, Luther, who are these people, how'd they get here?

Dead silence.

Pausing for a full twenty seconds, he then spun around responding with a question of his own.

"Have you ever wondered what happens to your garbage after you've left it on the curb, turned and headed back to your life? Think about it, we never really want to know what happens to all of the stuff that we've deemed useless. Our rubbish, our trash you see. Does it get ground up in some huge ball and twisted and compacted? Or does it get shoved into a red hot furnace and burned to a crisp? The rubbish has to end up somewhere, where do you expect it to go?"

But that doesn't answer my question, I returned. *And what's your story? How'd you get here and why are you still here?* I questioned.

Suddenly, out of the shadows rang an agonizing scream in woman's voice. Storming off in the direction of the screams, he hissed, "Shit, this wasn't supposed to be for another couple of weeks yet."

We caught up to find him leaning over a pregnant girl who was on her back reeling in pain. With her legs up and open it was easy to surmise that she was giving birth. Actually giving birth in this disgustingly filthy stall, like some stray dog in an old burned out tenement building. Rushing past us to reach the birthing mother was a charging old Black woman who appeared to be in her sixties. It was the first face that I was really able to see up close. She looked like my grandmother, and everyone else's. Standing off to the side we watched as the elder woman took charge, even calming down her patient. After walking away for a few paces, I turned and asked Luther, *Who's the pregnant girl?, how'd she get here?*

"We call her Little Sarah, real tragic story behind her curtain. She ain't but sixteen now, been here since she was twelve. When she was three years old she was rushed to this hospital because she could hardly breathe. Her entire windpipe was swollen almost shut. They later found out she had gonorrhea of the throat, at three years old. Seemed the momma's boyfriend had been forcing himself on the child, probably since her birth. Of course the mother couldn't believe such horrible things about her man. So further down in the depths of hell he'd drag Little Sarah as she would soon graduate to full penetration by the time she was six. Enduring unspeakable acts of sexual perversion, she soon grew to learn how despicable and loathsome her mother's live in lover really was. One day, not long after her eleventh birthday, she vowed never again to accept his advances, that she'd do any thing to defend herself. He made his last attempt one night when the mother was working late and Little Sarah was taking a bath. As he walked the long hallway to the bathroom eying the crack in the door for movement, he stripped himself bare. Sure that he was going to surprise her, he pushed the door open and popped his head in. What he didn't know was that she was waiting on the other side of the door with a surprise of her own, a sharp ax. The kid almost whacked his head off on the first swing. The second did the trick. After she severed his head, she cut off his prick. The story goes that once she started cutting she just couldn't stop; eventually hacking him into more than a thousand pieces. When the mother came home greeted by her blood soaked daughter, all she could think of was the whereabouts of her boyfriend. Little Sarah pleaded with her mother to believe her as she told her of the many years of sexual abuse at the hands of her so called step father. Calling her a tramp and a whore, that she was probably coming on to him, Sarah's mother completely shunned her, refusing to believe a word she said. Apparently it was too much for

Sarah, so she cut off her mother's head as well and then chopped her body into even smaller pieces than her first victim. Five days later they found her wondering around in the swamps some ten miles from the house, wearing the same bloody clothes she wore during the murders. They brought her here to the hospital for processing before taking her to jail. During her month long observation they found she was pregnant. She's been here having babies ever since, this is her fifth."

And no one missed her, no one at all, I asked.

"In this world, behind the walls of this institution absolutely anything is possible. Besides she was a throw away, who cared about her? She is the rubbish her parents left on the curb, when they turned to return to their lives. The hospital printed up a phony death certificate and declared her dead from complications during a difficult pregnancy. What you saw over there was a ghost, she doesn't exist. Her life, her soul, hell her ass belongs to."

Stopping short of saying who, he added, "Well, she no longer belongs to herself. Every one of these poor souls you see before you could tell you some of the strangest tales." He added with a twisted chuckle, "That is, if they still had their tongues. They're all throw- aways; society's human trash. Take that one over there, Mr. Foster, he's a half wit, hell truth be told the lot of them are half wits. Foster just started out stupid. They dropped him on his head as a baby or something. He's been around a good long while because he has a very rare blood type. They've already cut him open about six times. I'm surprised he's still breathing, he's missing so many organs." With a genuine look of surprise, he snapped, "Please forgive me for being so rude, and would either of you like something to eat?"

Not sure how to answer, I paused for a moment when Christine pulled at my pants leg, shaking her head yes. With that, I accepted his invitation. Fully half way into my meal, I chomped on the open flame grilled meat when something with a sharp point punctured the inside of my gum. Pulling the object from my gum, I continued to chew while I raised the object to the light of a torch. Without taking a second look, I knew immediately, what was stuck in my gum was the clawed hind foot of a rodent. Realizing that I had just eaten a rat, a tidal wave of bile rolled around my stomach, found my esophagus and erupted like Mt. St. Helen. Smacking his lips with approval while he ate, he shouted, "You know what they say, 'taste just like chicken'." Gagging and clutching my throat, I emptied my stomach on the spot. Finally able to talk, I wheezed, *I just need you to show me a way off the grounds, the sooner the better.*

Sarcastically he replied, "It's really a lovely place once you get used to it."

Well I'm not trying to get used to it, I'm trying to escape. Will you help us or not?

"Don't work yourself into a frenzy, I'll help you," he whispered.

I've got to stay on the move, we'd be on our way now if we knew our way around.

"Shit if you would," he retorted. "Even if you knew where to go you'd never make it. There's a series of underground catacombs that completely surround the compound. Through those catacombs travels the nastiest bunch of human garbage ever known to man. At one time they were just like you and me, they've been here for a long time, much longer than I've been. They tell me those creatures will strip a man whole, leaving the bones for the rats. They take the heads to the nest for the young to feed off the brain you know? The crazies that is, not the rats."

Continuing to amuse himself, he went on. "This fine institution is more than a hospital, it's more like a research center. All sorts of experiments are conducted here, and not just on the crazies. Some of them have less than thirty percent of their brain tissue left in their skulls. The mad scientists from above wanted to find out how the brain would process stored information with less and less brain tissue to work with. What they didn't count on was that the crazies would refuse to be handled. Going back to the animal within, they became extremely violent and no one could control them. I hear in the early days, the crazies killed more than a dozen orderlies and when they got their first taste of blood, it soon proved never to be enough. In no time the crazies began wandering the grounds mostly below, killing and eating anything living. They cost a hell of a lot of lives, but the good doctors from above didn't want to sacrifice their little lab animals. So they had them chased into the deepest corners of the catacombs with flame throwers, sealing them in with concrete walls. That happened more than thirty years ago and they say they've been breeding like rabbits. I know one thing from experience they are some fierce sons of bitches."

I'm sure you know they're not behind any wall anymore, I said.

"As they grew in numbers they started to outgrow their tiny underground world. When one got out, it didn't take long for the others to follow. Eventually the entire catacombs became their domain. No one knows where they make their nest, but there's so many of them that none of us would dare go through the tunnels alone. If you could make it through the catacombs and up to the grounds, you'd make it to freedom. The only problem, you'll never make it through the catacombs alive."

Still not willing to trust him with what I know about the catacombs I asked, *Then how the hell are you going to help?* Adding, *to listen to you, there's no way out of this hell hole.*

Puffing on the remains of an old cigar he scoffed, "I never said there was no way out, just that the catacombs would be suicide."

Damn it man, then how, how do we get the hell out of this mess? I demanded.

"How about a honeymoon for the misses, you could go on a cruise perhaps?"

What's that some kind of perverse joke? I snapped in anger.

"Tomorrow's the end of the month, time for the harvest," he quipped.

And what the hell is this, harvest? I asked.

"At the end of every month the 'Center' gathers up its bounty, in preparation for the harvest. They assemble a bunch of medicines and supplies, most donated by the hospital, but some of the local businesses contribute to the relief efforts the hospital is so famous for. They take regular trips to Bosnia, Europe, and some local island spots. With the supplies they add specimen samples of tissue and damaged organs for scientific research. While loading up the gear tomorrow, we could smuggle you and your lady on board. We make at least one stop in the Caribbean; we can drop you off at one of the islands."

I was still quite leery of Luther, and his plan. Perhaps it was easily read on my face.

He added, "This is a well respected operation that benefits countless thousands of people around the world, so I don't think we'll have any trouble once we get in open waters. Now does that sound like a perverse joke to you? Mr. well, you never did give me a name."

Dogan is my name, Wayne Dogan. The plan sounds like music to my ears, thanks for your help, I won't forget it.

"No need in thanking me yet, we get you and the misses safely ashore, then thank me. We've got a big day tomorrow, maybe you should let your woman get some sleep, looks like you could use some sleep yourself. The kid will show you where."

He began to walk away, but stopped, turning around with a crocked grin, he added, "See you on the other side."

He then turned and walked off, fading into the flickering shadows in the distance. Following Nathaniel to a dry empty spot on the dirt floor, we stopped to make our quick camp. With Christine fast asleep against my arm, I tried to sleep myself, but couldn't. Hardly able to believe that freedom could be so close at hand, I continued mightily to control my anxieties, forcing myself to get some rest. I laid still, in silence. On reflection of the challenges that besieged my existence since this nightmare began, I prayed to God that this may be the end. I prayed to God that I may rest in peace, one way or the other.....

Chapter 20

"Reaping the Harvest"

After lying down for not more than an hour, I soon rose to my feet unable or unwilling to sleep. Remembering the path I was taking I began to wander around in the sweltering heat. Covered in sweat, I squinted through stinging eyes while taking in the flurry of bodies that continued to scuffle about. Finally stumbling onto what Luther had previously called, "Ground Zero," I watched from a few feet away from the entrance. Not satisfied with my vantage point, I moved in closer, just outside of the chamber. Inside the deep chamber were seated at least a couple hundred people. Most were completely naked, while others wore little more than rags. At the feet of each of them were leg irons. Chained both, from one ankle to the other and chained to the person on their left and right. As far as my eyes could see, the cavern was littered with human cattle. They all stared down or up, almost never making eye contact with any of the others. With a far off look in their faces, they seemed broken. Suddenly, with the clarity of a hammer striking a bell, I knew instantly. I knew, at that moment that what I was witnessing was the real meaning behind my nightmare. Only it wasn't my nightmare alone. What I was witnessing, was the reaping of the harvest.

Overwhelmed by this gut-wrenching discovery, I fell to the ground, dizzy with torturous heartbreak. It was as if I'd jumped back in time to when the hideousness of the slave trade was commonplace. Just like the American slaves of yesteryear, they too it seemed were treated like animals, like the human property they are. In one glance I watched the evolution of the Negro in America as it was making its final turn to the three hundredth and sixtieth degree. In the wickedest of irony I thought, *we came here in bondage, in fear, in pain and in chains, and here we are three hundred years later, going out the very same way.* At that moment thoughts of my own freedom seemed small and selfish in comparison to my hopes for theirs.

Helping me to my feet with a scolding voice was a stone faced Luther.

"What are you doing here? you're suppose to be asleep with your lady. Now who's protecting her? Did you ever stop to think of that, Mr. Curiosity?" he taunted.

Realizing he was right, I told him so and began to make my way back to our bunking area.

"Hold on there, what's the rush? She's ok, besides the kid would be right here to tell me if something had happened," he tried to assure me.

No, I responded, *I want to see for myself to be sure she's alright.*

"Fine," he said, "I'll walk with you so you don't get lost."

First giving instructions to another man who carried a large paddle, presumably to keep the slaves in line, he then hustled back to where I was standing

"Let's go," he said, adding, "What did you think you saw back there?"

What the hell do you think I think I saw, I responded sarcastically.

"Fair enough," he said. "I think you saw something that you probably don't understand."

I understand all too well, they're selling slaves. Men, women and children, hell they're even breeding them like livestock. And they are all black, just like you, just like me. What else do I need to understand? I'm sure I've got a good grasp of what's happening here.

"I'm sure you don't, or at least you have an incomplete one."

I'll give you that, I don't have the complete picture, I don't know how you fit in here. What's your story and how'd you get here? More importantly, why do you stay?

"I'm what the courts call a habitual, serial rapist. It's been my problem since I was a kid. When I saw a woman that I liked it didn't matter if she liked me or not, if I decided that I had to have her, then I'd snatch her. I thought I had gotten control of it, until I almost got caught. When that happened it seemed to intensify the rush that I got from raping. So I kept doing it, all over the country. Then I got caught. The demons in my mind quieted down a little, mostly because there were no women around to speak of. Kicking around from prison to prison I began to meet other sex offenders, killers, child molesters, you name it. Boy did they put my stories to shame; they were in leagues all by themselves. Eventually I became hardened, more even, than when I was on the outside. Inside was where I vowed to add murder and torture to my repertoire, to see if it was all that my new friends made it out to be. At that point I had served four years of a fifteen-year bid, and I was already going out of my mind. Just months later, I got an early parole due to prison overcrowding, thank God for drug dealers. I eventually made my way down to the great racist state of Florida, more specifically Daytona Beach. It was so easy. The white girls were too ashamed to admit they had been raped by a Black man, you know the stigma and all. And nobody gave a shit about the Black girls so I almost never had anything to worry about. According to my shrink, it was my new lust for blood that eventually did me in. I must have flipped and started kidnapping women, at least two a month. I couldn't help it, I raped them, beat them and sometimes cut them up."

With the corners of his mouth curling into a smile, he continued. "Those were the good old days. After having a good run, I slipped up and made a mistake. I grabbed this one chick that I planned to kill, somehow she got away. Come to find out she was the daughter of some Jewish big shot judge, yeah, I hit the jackpot there. When they caught me they started talking about the death penalty on the first day. Even my court appointed mouth piece told me that if I copped to at least a dozen of the attacks he would see to it that I got no more than two life sentences. Not much of a choice, slow death verses the agonizing wait for the 'dead man's walk'. In a split second, I decided that I didn't like the choices that I'd opt for something else. I asked him why we couldn't plead insanity. He said because all of my crimes contained forethought, that they were premeditated. He said the only thing that would help in an insanity defense, would be to kill one of my visitors or something. Taking him seriously, I responded, 'but I don't have any one visiting'? Not knowing who he was dealing with he said, 'use your imagination,' putting his head back down into a clutter of papers on the table. Far be it from me not to take the advice of my counsel, so I used my imagination. I borrowed that fancy pen that he was so fond of, and before he knew it, I jabbed it into his eye. Then I jabbed it into his throat, about ten times. By the time the guards returned, his blood was everywhere; on the ceiling, all over the walls and floor, even on my face and in my mouth. I thought if I bit his ear off they would really know that I was certified crazy. After restraining me, they strapped on a straight jacket, from there, I just played the part that everyone wanted to believe in. Immediately they put me into solitary confinement. After a month in the hole, they brought me to this place. They played all kinds of head games. I supposed they had to try some of those textbook theories they learned about. I had the crazy act down to a science, fooling all but one of the doctors. I could never fool Dr. Michaels. The funny thing is he was chief of staff; not psychology. He started to sit down with me for two hour sessions everyday. He turned me inside out, and in no time he seemed to know me better than I knew myself. He soon told me what I was all about. He further told me what motivated me to rape, and why I needed to mutilate my victims. I asked him if I could ever be cured, he said flatly, 'no.' He then shocked the hell out of me when he said he may need someone with my particular qualifications. Of course my head was completely scrambled, and like a drowning man I knew I'd cling to even a rock if it were within my grasp. He told me how he had this operation. He didn't' tell me about the 'Harvest,' I kind of discovered it, much like you. Eventually I found out that Dr. Michaels has some kind of deal with the Russian mafia. They say they don't have much money, but they do have large stockpiles of weapons, which Michaels can sell without ever touching the goods. The Russian mafia on the other end sells organs that Dr. Michaels has harvested. Although there is a huge amount of money involved, it's nothing as compared to the live body market. Slaves today fetch a much better profit than they did in the sixteen hundreds. I suppose that's the long version of my story and how I got here. As to the question of why I stay. I suppose part of that is obvious. I'm a ghost too, just like Little Sarah. I'm part of that collection of society's human garbage pool, where would I go if I left here? Besides, why would I leave all of this? When I was on the outside I was always running from the law because I couldn't stop raping. In here rape is my job. I corral, feed, clothe and bathe all the females that come through here. They like their females pregnant, so I make a living screwing. Besides they politely told me that as long as I remained here nothing would happen to my parents, who are up there in years but they both are still very much alive. I'd like to keep it that way. I sure didn't make life any easier for them, the last thing I want to do is be the cause of their deaths. Who knows, I may just wait until we set sail and then turn them all loose. I've thought about it in the past, but I always stopped myself, fearing that they'd only bring my parents here so I could watch while they killed them. Then of course, they'd kill me too."

Astonishingly, he actually wiped a falling tear from his eye. After having paused for a while to listen to his story, we resumed our trek back to Christine and the boy.

So let me get this straight, I said. *These modern slave traders are capturing our people, selling them into bondage, and stealing organs from the weak and infirmed. You then take an active part in the breeding of humans for sale and experimentation and you want me to believe that you're somehow a victim in all of this; you've got to be kidding me? Where are they getting these people anyway?* I added.

"The homeless, accident cases, prisons, and mental hospitals you can take your pick. The world has no shortage of forgotten, useless, throw away people. Ask yourself how you got here, with no one on the outside having a clue as to where you are."

Pondering that thought, I felt the familiar pangs of anxiety as we made it back to where Christine was suppose to be. As I traced my steps back to the very spot, I found she and Nathaniel were gone. Panic-stricken, I grabbed Luther by his collar, pushing him up against a cavern wall.

Where are they, you sick son of a bitch? I demanded.

As he frowned and shrugged his shoulders as if to say he didn't know, I said, "*I'm not going to ask again.*"

With that he broke free of my grip, responding, "I'm not sure, I was with you remember? But there is one place we can check. Follow me closely, and don't lag behind."

After about ten brisk steps he stopped dead in his tracks and said, "You know I've decided. When we get out to sea I'm going to set all my brothers and sisters free, yeah, that's what I'm going to do."

Continuing on through the twisting caverns we eventually made it back to the staging area on the beach. There we were greeted with shouts coming from the men who were under Luther's control. Ever present was that all too familiar horrible crackling sound of that biting whip. By the time we made it to the clearing, they had already begun boarding. With supplies and specimen containers lining the wooden plank walkway, parading in a column of two's was a long and sickening line of doomed souls. More than a hundred boarded in just the few minutes that it took for Luther to ask two of his 'shepherds', as he called them, if either of them had seen Christine or the kid. With no's all around, I couldn't help but feel the agony that silently called from the bowels of the huge ship that seemed to just gobble up hundreds of chained dark bodies. As the clamor of metal shackles filled my ears, the pungent order of hundreds of sweaty bodies began to escape from the belly of the ship. Growing more afraid, I began to call Christine by name. *Christy, I shouted, where are you?* Now about ten yards in front of Luther, I continued to call with my back to him. Suddenly he shouted, "I think I found what you're looking for Mr. Dogan." Spinning around with relief, I turned expecting a tearful reunion, only to find that two of his henchmen were tightly clutching both Christine and Nathaniel by the throat. Not more than two steps in their direction, I was hit from behind, and everything faded to black.

When I awoke I found myself imprisoned in a cramped square shaped animal cage. With a flat top and steel bars all around, I wasn't going anywhere. I could see that I was no longer on the beach, but I had no idea where I was at that point. In the dim light I could see the hideously distorted figures of what must be a few crazies, trapped in their own individual cages. On the floor of their cage they each laid motionless, no doubt they'd been tranquilized or something. My last meeting with them found their actions to be anything but tranquil. Still groggy, I sat upright in my cage in anticipation of what was to come. Pondering the thought that Christine could be hundreds of miles away by now, I sat quietly in isolation.

Soon after, I began to hear something off in the distance. Now on my back, my hazy eyes were fixed on the ceiling of my cage. Now able to see, I focused in on the cage closest to me that housed one of the crazies. As my eyes further analyzed the cage and its steel bars, they stopped cold. My new vantage point left me petrified. The bars were totally mangled and twisted right out of their metal posts. The floor of the cage was barren. Its former prisoner was nowhere to be found. My heart was in my throat and the tension in my chest was about to explode. Growing in the back of me was a strange hissing sound, hissing, hissing then growling, and barking. Spinning around in horror, my face was pelted with heavy saliva as the barking continued. With both fists tightly gripping the bars on the outside of my cage, the thing on the other side panted, as it stared straight at me. Making eye contact with me at all times, the thing began to sway back and forth, back and forth. Then finally in a violent rage, it began to shake the cage; eventually shaking so hard that the cage rolled over on its side. In no time the heavy creature was on top, clawing his way through the steel bars, all the while shouting and grunting and squealing. Much to my horror, I soon discovered that the noise had awakened the other members of its clan. Hoping they were all still in their cages, I knew it would only be a matter of time before they all climbed out of theirs, and into mine. With nothing left to do but yell and scream, I continued to do a lot of both. Chiming in with the sentiment of my attacker, the others began to aggressively attack their cages. *My God,* I thought, *I never could have imagined such an ugly way to die. Never could I have known that I'd fall prey to cannibals. Nothing prepares you for being eaten. Oh my God, what the hell do I do now Lord?* Finally it stopped rattling my cage. The creature stopped, it seemed only to get a better grip of the bars. This was it. And this time, I was sure. Continuing to stare at me with those piercing eyes, the hideous monster began to grin with delight as the bars began to give way to his strength. Directly below his dripping saliva, I made my peace with God, while trying desperately to find the strength to accept my fate. I was completely humbled with terror. With my eyes closed and my spirit crushed, I bowed my head and began to pray. Suddenly the noise began to lessen, and in an instant, all was quiet. With dull thumps, they all began falling to the floor of their cages; including my attacker whose limp arm continued to hang through the bars, but inches above my head. In the blink of an eye the chaotic certainty of a most horrifying death, had been reduced to complete silence. Broken eventually by a scoffing Luther, "Looks like you met up with the crazies after all Mr. Dogan." His two flanking shepherds pulled the creature's sleeping body from the top of my cage, placing shackles on its wrists and ankles before throwing it into an empty cage. It seemed that during the height of their tantrum, Luther and his men heard the commotion, responding with tranquilizer guns. And in an odd twist of fate, I found myself happy to see Luther. What a hollow victory it is when one is saved from the jaws of death only to be delivered to the awaiting arms of his slave master. Now one nightmare ends just so that I may finish out another. Still totally unable to move a muscle, I sat there as the two prepared to move my cage. Standing the cage upright, I fell back into place with a thump. As they lifting from both ends I was now on the move. I soon found that I was on board the ship all the while. My seemingly lengthy slumber was really only about an hour or two. Having glanced at Luther's wrist watch, I saw that it was just about noon. When the men stopped, finding their destination they sat my cage directly in the midday sun. All around me was a flurry of activity, as the workers busily scurried to bring aboard the remaining boxes of supplies.

"Excellent," replied Luther, "we're almost there." Bending over a bit to look me in the eye, he said, "You're almost there too."

Luther, I called.

"What the hell do you want?"

I'd like to know why? Why did you betray us?

"Don't you get it yet fool? You were supposed to be the new rooster. That's what Dr. Michaels had planned for you, but not anymore. I'm the head rooster, the big man, the head nigger in charge. You would have had all of this lovely flesh to yourself. Imagine you could screw five times a day for every day of the rest of your life and never hit the same bitch twice."

Violently, he laughed at his own words as he raised a half gallon bottle of cheap wine to his lips. Already beginning to slur his words, he added, "That's right you dumb son of bitch, all you had to do was roll with the punches. Instead you decided you had to be a hero. I don't owe you shit boy.

What makes you think that I have to keep promises to you. I'm the head nigger and that's the way it's going to stay."

In strutted a calm, cool Dr. Michaels, fist making his way up the metal staircase then onto the deck of the ship. He marched straight up to my cage, bending himself to do as Luther did. With his usual biting sarcasm he quipped, "I had a job for you, if you didn't want it all you had to do was decline, I would have found something else for you." With a half hearted-chuckle he added, "You mean to tell me, this wasn't your boyhood dream job. Offer you a job doing nothing but porking the sweet flesh of the female animal, and you throw it back in my face. Well it is a dirty job and I guess someone has to do it, I guess it'll continue to be Luther." Walking completely around the cage he added, "What an excellent physical specimen you are. You've shown that you are quite intelligent and cunning as well. Yes, I do like that, what a waste."

Leaning further towards the cage, his hands now reaching in, he grabbed me around the front of my shirt saying, "You damned fool all you had to do was go along. We can't be beaten, don't you know that by now. How could you be so smart and so dumb at the same time?"

Letting me go, but not before smacking me in the front of my head he said, "I've been mildly amused by your tenacity, under different circumstances, I would even applaud it, but as all things must come to an end, so too must you.... Have a good swim."

Turning his back on me he shouted to Luther, "You can do what ever you choose with the girl, but wait until you're at least two days at sea then feed him to the sharks." He then picked up his stroll across the deck of the ship with his arm on Luther's shoulder. Luther then began taunting me as he dragged Christine by a rope, firmly knotted around her neck. As Dr. Michaels made his way over to the captain, he told Luther to obey the captain and he'd be permitted to return after they delivered the harvest. After forcing

Christine on her knees, he said he would obey the captain and leaned forward as Dr. Michaels patted him on his head saying, "Good boy." Dr. Michaels then walked off with the captain, spoke a few final words, turned with a half hearted salute in my direction and departed the ship. Out of the corner of my eye, I caught the glimpse of Nathaniel's small frame, he was free. Hiding under a pile of ropes and supplies, he'd done as he had been doing all along, avoiding capture. Seeing him was just the ray of hope that I needed.

Meanwhile, Luther dispatched six of his shepherds to untie the line from the dock post. Lifting the anchor they helped guide the captain out of the narrow slip. Afterwards, he ordered them to report to their posts. He then began to strut across the length of the deck, crowing like a rooster. With Christine, firmly clinched within the tightening grip of his rope, he continued his backwards stroll while grinning still at me. With her hands tied behind her back, his left hand choking his victim, and his right firmly grasping between her legs, he began to disappear out of sight, presumably to make ready to mount his new bitch, my wife— my soul-mate. He may as well have mounted me. With crushing pain, this scene ripped my insides bare. There my mind exploded into a thousand pieces, and suddenly I was no longer there. Somehow managing to sit upright, I faded deeper into the spiraling circles in my mind. I'd never felt so hollow. I was entirely empty.

Vaguely noticing the jingling sound in the front of my cage, I continued to escape to far off unknown places. Only the sound of the latch springing open with a small bang, did I begin to come out of my trance. Like a typical kid trying to coax an animal out of a cage, standing in front of me was a sopping wet ten year old dressed like a monk. Waving his hand towards himself, he said, "Luther down below, I show you, come on." Forcing myself to gather my selves together, I stepped out of the cage, into the pouring rain. As we started for the staircase, I turned to look again at that hideous cage. Knowing I just had to, I reached for a firm grip of the bars and pulled the cage toward the starboard bow. With the ship slamming boisterously into the waves, and the spray just about to raise me off my feet, I abandoned the idea of tossing the cage overboard. We quickly made our way to the staircase. Making it to the first lower level, Nathaniel took the lead. First, passing me a home-made knife that was more like an ice pick, he then stopped and turned to speak in his familiar tongue-less garbled voice.

"I didn't know Luther wanted to hurt you. He told me it was a game. You know like a maze. He told me if I could find you through the vents then he would take me home. I'm sorry," he whimpered, "Honestly I am, I didn't know."

I know you didn't know, I responded, *no one knew any of this could be possible.* Adding, *you've saved my life more than once, trust me I know your heart's in the right place.* He smiled and resumed his course. Although the ship was huge and carrying almost a thousand slaves, the crew was surprisingly small. Including the captain, his crew, Luther and his ten shepherds, there were only about two dozen of them. I felt surely we could overpower such a small group, take the ship and free the rest of the slaves. The first order of business however was to find Christine, then Luther and kill him. I could have breathed fire at that point, I was out for blood. Following Nathaniel's lead with the shank in my hand, I stopped short of running him over as he abruptly stopped and pointed to a green door with the shape of a rooster carved in it. There was no doubt as to whose quarters this was. With the knife in my left hand, I twisted the knob with my right. Slowly I opened the door. Inside it was like some kind of makeshift torture chamber. With metal contraptions, benches with restraining brackets and other assorted pain givers, I scanned the large room for movement. As we stepped inside, the sound of running water grew louder. Inside a tiny bathroom bounced the shadow of what appeared to be Luther. *If he's in there, then where is Christine?* I thought. Hearing the faint muffle of a cry for help, Nathaniel zipped over to a small closed door, which turned out to be a closet. Inside was a terrified Christine. Her hands were still tied behind her back, her mouth gagged, and her clothes removed. She was fastened to some sort of wooden gallows, where she was bent into a position of sexual submission with her legs spread apart. Assuming that I was too late, that he had already raped her, I charged the bathroom like a bull. Hearing the commotion, Luther rushed to the bathroom door, where I lunged forward in his direction. With a surprising amount of ease, the blade sliced through his flesh, like a hot knife through butter. The look of surprised terror on Luther's face was so rewarding that I pulled the knife from his belly and stabbed him again, this time in the chest, then in the throat. By the time I was through, his blood was everywhere. There was blood on the walls, all over the floor and even the ceiling. I showed the treacherous rapist no mercy, cursing and kicking his lifeless carcass. Drenched in Luther's blood, I soon turned my attention to Christine. First removing the gag from her mouth, I then freed her from the strange contraption, asking her if she was ok. Again, Nathaniel turned over his hooded robe— of which I dressed Christine. She said he tried to rape her, but she scratched him badly across the eyes. Finally, he decided to pin her down on this wooden horse like device, he then disappeared into the washroom moments before we came in. Crying tears of pain and joy, she said, "I wouldn't give in honey, just like you taught me, I didn't give in." Collapsing to the floor, she passed out. After dragging Luther's body into the closet, I closed the door and looked for a soft place to hide Christine. Not finding one, I settled for the shower in the bathroom. Closing its door, we looked around for anything that could be used as a weapon. Arming ourselves with a couple of metal pipes plus the knife, we set out to find the slave quarters to free them. By the time we'd made our way to the cramped slave quarters, we found they had started a revolt on their own. The noise was deafening, overpowered only by the smell. It seems the killing started not long after setting sail, which could not have been by accident. Running into one of Luther's shepherds, I readied myself for a fight.

"You don't want to fight me," he said, "your fight is with Luther. We don't have time for long stories, but I've hated that sadistic son of a bitch since I've pulled this hell bound duty, by the way I'm Ramsey."

Putting his hand out to shake mine he said, "You can believe me, this revolt was a long time in coming and I planned it right. All we have to do now is kill that rotten ass Luther and stop the captain from making a ship to shore call," he said.

Well we don't have to worry about Luther any more, he's finished, I said.

"You mean finished as in dead?" he asked.

Completely finished, entirely dead, I answered.

"Then I guess it's true after all?"

What's true?

"That you some kind of superman. Slippery. Boy, Dr. Michaels hated your ass something fierce. Did you know that boy?"

First of all, I ain't your boy and I don't give a fuck about Dr. Michaels, you neither. You are one of Luther's so called shepherds, aren't you?

"True enough, I am. I mean, I was, and I'm sorry about that. But you have to understand."

I interrupted; *I don't have to understand shit you have to understand what has happened to me and my wife since we've been in that insane asylum. If I live to be a hundred, I'll never forget it, and I'll never forgive anyone who made any of this madness possible. That includes you, so if you don't want to die, stay the hell away from me, my wife and the kid.*

"You got things all wrong. I'm not the man you think I am. I'm nothing like Luther, I hated that drunken ass pervert."

Then what the hell are you doing here?

"I'm only here because my daughter needed a kidney transplant. She was coming to the end of her rope and her number on the donor register was so high, you know how it is, black and poor, the double whammy. Anyway, Luther was bragging at a bar one night about how he could get me any organ I needed. I was desperate, so I took him up on it. He told me when to have Jenny, that's my daughter, to the hospital that he'd take care of everything. Miraculously they told me right on the spot that they had found a match just that quick Jenny was going to live. They prepped her for surgery, making all the necessary arrangements and such, then Luther called me over and told me to follow him. That was the first time I had been introduced to the janitors' closet. All through the catacombs, he showed me the whole operation. That was when I knew my life was over. The cost of my Jenny's life was to give my own life in return. Yeah they talked about this indentured servant crap, but believe me, once you've seen the operation, they'd never let you out alive. They actually said they only needed me to work here for three years, which was almost five years ago. I've hated every day of this filth, but I don't regret anything, and I'd do it again if I had to."

Have you ever seen your daughter since? I asked.

With a wide grin he said, "Yeah I've seen her. She does volunteer work at the hospital sometimes." Turning stern faced and gloomy he added, "But they don't let me talk to her. They say if ever I told her about their work, they'd include her and kill my wife and son. She doesn't even know I'm alive. My entire family thinks I walked out on them. Tears me up but she's alive and that's all that counts. Besides, once they showed me the operation, their offer was one that I could not refuse, even if I wanted to. That's the real story. And you know what every one of Luther's shepherds has a similar story to tell."

Maybe I'll get to tell you my story one day, you'll have to set aside a few days though. But right now, I'm on my way back to get my wife. Taking a few steps I turned and asked, *well, you coming?*

With that familiar wide grin he answered, "Yes, I'm coming."

It seemed the other shepherds didn't fare so well. On the way back to Luther's cabin we saw a few running from a mob, and stepped over the body of another. We made it safely back to the cabin where Christine was preparing herself for battle. She'd found a small hand ax, a few more pipes and even some food. With a cloth bandana around her head to keep her hair out of her face, and ax in hand, she was ready. I went to introduce her to Ramsey she responded coldly, "I know who he is. Keep him away from me or I'll kill him." The look in her eyes and the strength in her voice told me and Ramsey that she was deadly serious. So I told him it may be wise to keep his distance. He agreed. By the end of the day scores of freed slaves were dead or injured. All of Luther's shepherds were dead except for Ramsey. Every crew member who wasn't vital to the operation of the ship was executed, right on the outside main deck. The death count was now at twenty and still rising. Except for the captain and the engine crew, all other crew members died in the most dreadful ways. At least for that moment, this ship of shackled slaves had been turned into one that carried newly freed ones. With their new freedom came hope. But for most, it seemed to fuel their hatred for their former captors. Filled with the unquenchable thirst for blood and vengeance, we continued to head straight out into the open sea. There we forced the captain to maintain his course in route for the original destination. The former Soviet Union, now the Baltic States. Once there we planned to liberate our brothers and sisters, and expose the slave traders to the local government officials. The Russian mafia, it seemed had organized the entire affair, a feeble attempt to rebuild the once mighty Soviet Union with slave labor.

Black slaves, from the Americas.....

Chapter 21

"The Final Journey"

We never did make it to the Baltic's. Things went a little haywire on the ship. Provisions ran low and some hard choices had to be made. Sickness spread like wild fire, perhaps because there wasn't much left to eat except the rats that completely infested the hull. Soon we became faced with the decision of whether or not to continue to waste food and water on the weak and sick. We stopped almost immediately after it was first proposed. With no medicine and very little supplies the mildly sick would soon become critical and die within days. We were losing at least a half dozen or more a day. That is, in the beginning. The worst was surely yet to come. While we didn't know exactly what happened to the crazies, we found out that at least ten were on board. And as usual, we were their prey.

The Captain, with all of his arrogance and irreverent behavior would strut around drunk as could be. Shouting orders to the, then free slaves, daring them to raise a hand to him. One afternoon the captain decided he would have his way with a thirteen year old slave girl. "Nigger Vermin," he'd say. Just as he was about to enter the little girl who was bent over the mahogany railing on the starboard side of the ship, he dropped to his knees. Clutching his chest he fell backwards, screaming in agonizing pain. He looked down as if in disbelief. His body was deeply punctured with four huge fish hooks, the ones with the pine tree styled heads designed to gut the huge tuna when removed from the fishes' mouth. At the end of each hook was a large o-ring which was attached to the first link in a very long chain. At the end of this great chain of about fifteen feet was a pair of hands. The hands belonged to Christine.

She then pulled the Captain away from the little girl. Further ripping his flesh, she tugged hard at the chain. As he wailed in pain, she dropped the chain to the deck, walked over to his bloody, contorted body and spit in his face. With her foot on his throat she reached down and yanked out the first hook. With a blood curdling scream the Captain wildly thrashed about as his blood sprayed all over Christine's face and body. Again she grabbed hold of a second hook and pulled with all of her might. With that she pulled out a large section of bone, his backbone had been snapped in two. Coughing up blood and spinal fluid, he gasped his last gurgling breath. Helping the little girl to her feet, Christine wiped the blood and tears from her face and took her below.

Like hyenas on a freshly stolen kill, about a dozen or so men lunged in on the body. Ripping it to pieces, they kicked and hammered and stabbed his badly mutilated body throughout the night. By morning the rats had eaten most of his flesh and you could barely tell that this clump of meat and bones was once a man. With the Captain dead and the ship now helplessly adrift, I knew it wouldn't take long before all hell would break loose.

We drifted for days. Rations were down to almost nothing and clean drinking water was more precious than gold. Everyone seemed to be losing their minds, including me. Fights to the death, broke out all over the ship. The women were being savagely raped and some were killed in the process. Like animals fighting over a drying water hole the men fought like savages; killing each other over rats and small corners of shade in order to escape the oppressive burning from the sun. The remaining white crew members were treated much like the Captain, but not until after being repeatedly gang raped and tortured. The bodies were then speared at the top of the main masts, one on top of the other. There, remained a constant cloud of vultures feeding off the bodies. There were so many vultures that occasionally a few would swoop down, landing on the deck. With all of the arrogance of a merchant of death, the huge menacing birds would calmly strut the wooden deck. Poised and ready, they began to take their feed of the sick and wounded long before they were actually dead. The original cargo of nearly one thousand people dwindled down to less than five hundred. This ship of horror was a disease-ridden, rat- infested bordello of rape, murder and degradation rarely recorded by man.

The remaining few hundred or so were the worst of the worst. Surviving based on the highest and most basic order, "Survival of the fittest." And on this ship to be the fittest is to be the most brutal, the most cunning and the most desperate to live. Many survived by banding together, which is how Christine and I had survived so long. *The kid?* The kid had more natural survival skills than the lot of us. Crawling through holes no one else could fit through, he would regularly escape the clutches of many of the gangs who had resulted to cannibalism. Those were the worst, next to the crazies of course. Children especially were deemed to be good eating. The kid had more trouble with rats than the gangs or crazies, as he would duck and hide into crevices. He would soon learn why his means of survival would become his eventual down fall. The crevices were often manned with posted sentries, strategically dispatched by groups of rats that also began to travel the ship in packs. Having been bitten more times than he could remember, the kid became quite proficient at killing even the largest and most ferocious rats. One time however, he wasn't so lucky.

One morning while traveling through drain pipes he inadvertently disturbed a nesting ground of some thirty or so nursing mother rats. Having crushed a few babies of the first rat that he encountered, he recoiled when he realized what he had done. Too late! In no time he was completely surrounded on all sides by hungry salivating rats. I imagined he fought with the greatest of fury, though unsuccessful this final fight. By the time we were able to remove a section of the pipe, out jumped hordes of rats as they scurried in every direction. What remained was one of the most sickening sights that I had seen yet. The rats not only stripped the boy clean, but managed to eat through bone. Taking with them rib bones, fingers and toes. Exhausted and sickened by the continuous onslaught of grief, I scraped up Nathaniel's remains, said a brief prayer and tossed what was left into the sea.

Seemingly suffering from malaria, or something like it, I struggled to go on. Fighting for my life each day, the will to live began to slip away fast. Totally mad out of her mind, Christine fought on. Fighting with the fury of the devil, she commanded respect from even the toughest gangs. With garbled speech she reminded me of the experiments that the doctors had performed on her. Recanting how they abused her and how she killed at least three orderlies. She swore to me that no one will ever do that to her again. That she would keep killing until there was no one else left to kill.

By now the ship was a floating cesspool. The walls and floors were covered with blood as body parts were generously thrown about the deck. Small fires were breaking out all over the ship and the vultures still hovered, waiting for signs of weakness.

The rats have all but overtaken the lowest two decks of the ship, where there was a feeding frenzy on the more than one hundred people trapped by the water that's been pouring in from the sea. Several holes in the ships bowels sealed the fate of this unholy vessel.

Punctured by a massive coral reef, the ship slowly began to sink. Furiously, I fought to clear my mind long enough to figure out what to do. With Christine, Ramsey and a few others by my side, we fought our way to the life boats. The boiler exploded in the engine room, and the ship began to tilt decidedly to one side. In a panic, many jumped over board. It was then that I realized another kind of feeding frenzy was going on in the water. More sharks than I thought existed were in the waters, greedily anticipating an easy meal. One by one our former shipmates jumped to their deaths, almost instantly being gobbled up whole. With sharks circling below, vultures circling above, fires raging out of control on all decks, people drowning while others were eaten alive by rats— the mayhem and murder continued. As we made our way to an emergency raft, Christine jumped in and motioned for me to lower the boat. Lowering the wooden craft into the water, I fought off my last assailant and jumped over the side. In and out of the water in seconds, I started the small motor as I called to Ramsey and the few that fought so tirelessly with us. They jumped in the water just within reach of the boat. I was able to pull Ramsey in and quickly returned to grab another. With his arms in my hands, I noticed that a large shark was approaching fast. The huge shark lunged forward scraping its large belly across the full length of the boat. With its cavernous mouth opened, exposing rows of jagged teeth, the shark ripped the man from the edge of the boat leaving me with both of his arms in my hands. His hands still firmly gripping my forearms, as the blood squirted profusely against the inner side of the boat. The other two in the water were taken down even quicker than the last. Exhausted, hungry and thirsty we headed out to sea without a speck of land in sight.

Hopelessly adrift, our skin burned from the intensity of the sun. Having taken total leave of our senses, expecting to die—we began feuding with each other. Finally, the other man with us, Ramsey, fell dead to the floor of the boat. Dead after having received several crushing blows to the head, delivered by both Christine and I. It seemed he wasn't as innocent as he first led me to believe. As Christine described how he stood back and cheered the orderlies on when they came to her room to molest her. Upon hearing that, I was unable to control my temper, and began to beat him for lying to me. With madness in our hearts and blood in our eyes we began to hack and dismember our enemy.

We devoured the warm salty flesh and swabbed up the blood like gravy in our hands. Licking our fingers and staring into each others eyes we broke into spontaneous laughter. Blood soaked and void of all humanity we looked down at the mangled, fly infested carcass. Slowly, we drifted off to sleep.....

Days later we were picked up by a salvage vessel. We were so far gone that we had no idea of what was going on. While on board we were nursed back to reasonable health while being held prisoner somewhere deep in the belly of the ship. It turned out that the salvage vessel was sent out to find the missing ship and her precious cargo; dispatched from that horrible hospital on the far eastern coast of Central Florida— The same one that we fought so hard to escape. It took very little time to reach land. It seems that we were never more than five hundred miles out of U.S. waters.

I was brought back to the dark, musty room where the monk-like figures congregated. There, I was found guilty of a long list of crimes against the Republic of Racial Purity in America. *My punishment? Death, by dismemberment.* Waiting and waiting for the final curtain to come crashing down, I sat in my dark, damp cell for what seemed like an eternity. *I never saw that curtain. Nor have I ever seen my freedom. My fate is one that no human should ever have to endure. Instead of instant death I've been locked in this drafty cell, high in the upper towers. Here is where I've been for the last sixteen years or so. It is here that I sit and watch this month's load of slaves being hustled aboard the large and curiously modern ship. From my gruesome perch, I am able to watch the most despicable business on the planet, the flesh trade. It's grown larger by the month; every month, for all of my years in this tower.*

I can't move around as well now, not since they cut off all my toes. They said that way I won't ever try to run again. The first night alone they cut out my tongue and left it on the floor of the cell. I assumed it was left there as a reminder— that I would never be able to tell my story. That may have been so however they had at least one additional thing in mind. Some two days later without food or water, I was told just what to do with the tongue. They said I won't eat again until I first eat my own tongue. I was so very hungry, so I ate it. It just reminded me of the time that Christine and I ate the raw, warm flesh of Ramsey, our lifeboat companion, only a little dryer and tougher. I guess, I've been a flesh eater ever since. I heard that Christine didn't make it, but then I've heard that before. Every time I convince myself that she could have gotten away, they torment me with body parts they say belonged to her. Just as well, I would hope she hasn't had to endure all that I've endured since our second capture, almost two decades ago. My mind is almost gone now, on account of all of the experiments and surgeries. I lost my right eye to a rat once as I slept, but I can still see pretty well out of my left eye. Good enough at least to write this sordid and ugly tale in the hopes that one day it'll all be over.

Eventually, I was rewarded with a job! You know, for good behavior.

My job?

My job is to dispose of the empty bodies after the organs have been harvested.

I like my job.

I'm quite grateful and you got to love the fringe benefits.

I get to eat all that's not good enough for the harvest.

Don't ever let anyone tell you that slavery doesn't exist.

I know different.

Don't ever let anyone tell you that hell doesn't exist.

It does.

They are both one in the same......

THE END!

And The Harvest continues......